MW01088966

GHOST DICK

A PORT CANYON CHRONICLE

KINSLEY KINCAID

Copyright © 2023 by Kinsley Kincaid

All rights reserved.

No part of this book may be reproduced in any form or by any electronic or mechanical means, including information storage and retrieval systems, without written permission from the author, except for the use of brief quotations in a book review.

This book and its contents are entirely a work of fiction. Any resemblance or similarities to names, characters, organizations, places, events, incidents, or real people are entirely coincidental or used fictitiously.

eBook ISBN: 978-1-7389892-8-7

Paperback ISBN: 978-1-7389892-9-4

Cover Design: HC Graphics

Editing and Proofreading: Book Witch Author Services

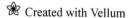 Created with Vellum

DISCLAIMER

Please be aware this book contains many **dark themes** and subjects that may be uncomfortable/unsuitable for some readers. This book contains **heavy themes** throughout. Please keep this in mind when entering Ghost Dick: A Port Canyon Chronicle. Content warnings are listed on authors' social pages & website.

This book and its contents are entirely a work of fiction. Any resemblance or similarities to names, characters, organizations, places, events, incidents, or real people are entirely coincidental or used fictitiously.

If you find any genuine errors, please reach out to the author directly to correct it. Thank you.

Please do not distribute this material. It is a criminal offence!
This book is intended for 18+ only.

To the OG Ghost Dick, Devon Sawa.
Can we keep you?

PLAYLIST

Tear You Apart - She Wants Revenge

Circus Psycho - Diggy Graves

your favorite dress - Lil Peep, Lil Tracy

E-GIRLS AND RUINING MY LIFE - CORPSE, Savage Ga$p

Moonlight Magic - Ashnikko

Whore - Get Scared

Halloween IV:Innards - Ashnikko

POLTERGEIST! - CORPSE, OmenXIII

you should see me in a crown - Billie Eilish

Bongos - Cardi B, Megan Thee Stallion

Spotify Playlist

Note from the Author

This is a Dark Halloween Taboo Story. The FMC &
MMC are very much related. You may get the urge to
punch them both in the face while reading. That's ok.
They probably deserve it a time or two? A few other
characters may as well. Don't limit yourself with your
throat punching.

Also!

Please keep in mind I've never had ghost sex, so how
I describe and interpret it could be different from
what you have experienced in similar circumstances.
You may say, 'This isn't realistic'. But to Merrick and
Fallon, it very much is. To the town of Port Canyon,
it's just another day.

You may finish reading this hoping a ghost visits you

tonight and I fucking hope your dreams come true, Queens. You deserve any type of delicious, panty soaking experience you desire.

Enjoy!
-Kins

PORT CANYON

Isolated deep within the wild mountains of Washington State, Port Canyon is very much like most historic towns; cobblestone roadways lined with natural stone-front shops and a rustic clock tower features prominently in the town square. Relatively untouched by modernization, many of its buildings are unchanged since it was first settled in the 1800s. Filled with Victorian castle-like estates, some decorated in a dark gothic style, and completed by brightly light cottages covered in vines. Nothing about Port Canyon is new, less than nothing about it is normal.

Outside of Halloween, you will rarely find visitors roaming the town. New residents are few and far between. Fallon is the first new arrival in recent memory, and she's never heard the tales of Port

Canyon. Tales full of more truth than lies. She wouldn't be here unless she had to be. Even the reasons for it are hidden behind another. Layered to protect the town.

Her grandmother is one of the few residents whose bloodline is left. She's been alone for years.

Like every generation before her, Grandma Joanie is the keeper of the graveyard. She helps the newly dead to adjust to their new reality, keeping them happy and safe as they make a peaceful transition. Forced to live with her grandmother, Fallon will soon learn what it means to be the keeper of the Port Canyon graveyard.

Other families who call Port Canyon home are very protective of their secluded little town. They are the ones who keep the legacies and legends alive. You will briefly meet them here, although this is not their story. This is the story of the graveyard, its keeper, its residents and their legacies.

The Graveyard is where this story calls home.

There will definitely be ghosts... and plenty of one in particular.

Welcome to Port Canyon.

MERRICK

PROLOGUE

20 YEARS OLD - PORT CANYON 1985

*S*hifting gears, I can hear the roar of the engine. It matches the vibration rumbling through my body. It's the only thing my brain registers. I know this road like the back of my hand, day or night, I could drive it with my eyes closed. It's after midnight, and the clouds only allow some of the moonlight to shine through. A low fog winds its way through the forest, rolling up within the tree line on either side of the road. I'm driving to escape. I'm twenty years old, and I'm running away from my fucking mommy issues. Lingering since birth, this is nothing new. You don't choose who your parents are. You don't choose the life you're born into. Your fate *has been written for you. There is nothing you can do to change it.*

My dad passed away a few years ago. He just didn't wake up one morning, lucky bastard. Since then, everything has gotten worse. Her duty has become an obsession. If you even so much as whisper about it, she'll explode. It always turns into a fucking battle with that woman.

Dad came here one Halloween with his friends when he was nineteen, took one look at my mom and never left. That shit's rare. Outsiders rarely come here, or even consider moving here. He had no idea what he was getting into. Fuck. I miss him.

Always the voice of reason. He was the best dad.

Out of sheer frustration, I slam my hands against the hard steering wheel of my burgundy Honda CRX. When will we ever be enough for her? When will she see we matter? We are her fucking kids! But she puts us on the goddamn back burner. For them.

We are responsible for them. We are responsible for keeping legacies alive, Merrick. It's why our family has remained in Port Canyon generation after generation.' It's always the same fucking thing.

Fuck you. Fuck the legacy. Fuck our generational responsibility. If I ever have kids, I'll never prioritize that shit over them. Never!

My younger brother, Mark, he sees it. He internalizes his feelings, but it showed in his clenched fists while his eyes scanned the small crowd in town center, realizing Mom was missing his graduation for them. It was when I knew he saw it without a doubt. In a small town like this his graduating class had all of ten students. A missing parent is noticed. I showed up.

Mark has to get out. He will get out.

I hold nothing back. Biting my tongue or filtering my words has never been an option. It's not my personality.

Shifting gears again, and reaching maximum speed, I approach the bridge separating Port Canyon from the rest of the world. My mind is made up.

That's another thing about me. I'm a stubborn fucker.

Mark. Read my words carefully in the morning.

Mom. Hear me loud and fucking clear. I'll never be trapped in this place.

Never and neither will Mark.

Taking one hand off the wheel, I rake my fingers through my white blond hair while blowing out a breath. It's go time.

Placing both hands back on the wheel, my car is cruising, the engine roaring with life as I crank my steering wheel hard to the right, never letting off the gas.

My front end breaks through the flimsy metal barrier towards the shallow, rocky water below, inky in the dead of night.

Fuck you, Port Canyon. I'll never be your prisoner.

CHAPTER 1
FALLON
PRESENT DAY

P ulling up to my grandmother's house in a car that once belonged to her now dead son, my dad, seems wrong. Especially since I've never met her. It took him ages to find the grand prix white 1985 Porsche 911 and fully restore it, but he was determined to get the 1985 model.

The year his brother died, combined with his favorite car. In a way, I think it helped him keep his brother's memory alive. To be close to him in those moments when he felt so far away. Maybe, I don't know. It's what makes the most sense.

Now both her sons are dead. And here I am, pulling up with memories of them on hand.

This isn't a surprise visit. She knows I'm coming. Her number was in my dad's cell phone, and I have nowhere else to go. My mom's somewhere, but no one actually knows where. She left us when I was still in diapers. I've seen her on and off over the years, but we have never been close. My parents had a hard time conceiving me. By the time I was finally born, she was halfway out the door. Fucking traitor. She's nothing more than someone who birthed me for my dad.

They said it was a brain aneurysm. He was awake one minute. Dead in the shower the next. Our weekly house cleaner found him.

We lived in a nice middle-class neighborhood in northern California. Dad had a good job. I never went without. I always had food to eat and the latest toy. Any activity I wanted to try, he would sign me up. He fucking loved me so much. And now all that's left of him are ashes, which are safely buckled next to me, boxes with photo albums and a few clothes that smell like him, and this car.

The bank took the house.

After going through all his stuff, they gave me two weeks to clean it out before putting it on the fore-closure block. I found overdue notices for the mort-gage and bills that had been sent to collectors. Turns out that he still loved my mom all these years later because I also found a notebook listing all the times he wired her money. Dad was giving her cash when-ever and for whatever she needed. Cash he didn't have. I had no idea. Was she more important to him than staying with me?

I know no one could have predicted this. But it doesn't stop a person from wondering what, if, or why? So many unanswered questions are left for the ones who survive.

There's nothing that can be done now, he's gone.

So here I am, in my dead dad's vintage Porsche in my grandmother's driveway in Port fucking Canyon, Washington.

It's a big difference from California. The sun barely shines here, no matter what season. The people I've seen while driving through town are pale and creepy.

I already hate it here. Tears well in my eyes. There's nowhere else to go. College is out of the question. Can't afford it and I have no idea what I want to be when I grow up. I'm only twenty. Still confused about adulting, but since dad died, it's even more so.

What is my purpose?

There's no way anyone's going to find it here. This feels like a place people come to die, not live.

Looking up from my grip on the leather steering

wheel, I decide it's time to go in and face what is coming. Maybe my soul will die here too and there will be no need to figure out what's next.

Looking around the property through the windshield, I see Grandma Joanie, who is shorter than I imagined, maybe five feet to my five three, so that's who I get my height from. She's wearing a cream summer dress that has a swooping neckline and cinches at the waist with short sleeves. It's long and goes all the way down to her feet, which look like they are clad in fuzzy pink slippers. Her body is curvy, fingers full of rings and wrists covered in bracelets. A black diamond or some sort of crystal, a cross necklace hangs around her neck. Her hair is white, short just above the ears and full of natural curls. Joanie is standing on the wraparound porch. Fuck. How long has she been out here? Watching me? Why hasn't she come over? Creepy old lady, just like the rest of the godforsaken place. Fuck.

Looking behind her, I take in the massive gothic mansion I'll be calling home. Black and white roses line the cobblestone pathway leading from the driveway to the house. Everything is black. From the wood of the stairs, to the wraparound porch and iron railings. There are at least three stories of black brick that match the shingles covering the gabled roof. The porch is covered the entire way around the house. I have to crane my neck back to see the entirety of the tall tower in the middle of the house; it surpasses the rest of the home's peaks and seems to touch the sky from all the way down here. There is a glass door on the second floor terrace and a small window at the top with a pointed arch above. I think it even has a cross at the top of the pointed arch. My new home reminds me of a castle. Small windows line the top floor with the same arches encasing them, and large three-story bay windows trimmed in black, balance the sides of the front door. The double front door matches the height of the sentinel windows and is the same shade of black, with a gold door knocker, peep-hole and knob standing in stark contrast to the darkness.

I had to drive through mile-high iron gates to get here, and the same skull with a filigree emblem that was on the gate is on the enormous door. The long, paved driveway twisted and turned through acres of surrounding forest on the way to the secluded monstrosity. She has to be loaded. It's the only expla-nation. How else can she afford this place? It's like a mansion. An old, creepy, dark mansion.

Which makes me wonder. Why wouldn't dad ask her for help? Maybe the same reason I've never met her? Which I also don't know the answer to, but the excuses aren't something I'm interested in.

Joanie is still watching me. She hasn't moved from her spot on the porch. Not even a wave or a smile from her.

Rolling my eyes, I drop my head against the head-rest of my seat and decide it's time to get this over with.

You can do it. Come on, Fallon, just make the best out of a terrible situation. It's this or you live in this car.

Maybe I should have picked the car.

Dammit. It's too late now. She's seen me. I'm here.

Time to get this family reunion over with.

CHAPTER 2

FALLON

S lamming my car door shut, I take in one last deep breath, trying to steady my already shot nerves. I'm exhausted and orphaned, and this woman who is my grandmother can't even be bothered to come to my car to meet me? To grab her dead son from my passenger seat. Arm too fucking tired to wave?

Damn.

First impressions at this point are not great. I'm not exactly feeling the warm and fuzzies you'd typically expect from grandmothers. This is far from what I've seen on television or what my friends have told me.

My friends' grandparents would spoil them. Overwhelm them with attention. They'd text me saying *'save me', 'send help'* or *'I swear my gramps doesn't get that I'm a teenager. Kissing on the lips isn't ok anymore.'* They would complain about the old person's smell lingering, which always made me laugh too.

Sometimes I wished I had experienced those things, but my dad was always enough for me.

Shaking my head to clear it of the memories, and looking over to the porch again, I find Grandma Joanie is still standing there, watching me. It's getting creepy and slightly uncomfortable.

Screw it. Let her wait a bit longer.

Miserable old shrew.

Walking to the other side of my car, I open the door, unbuckle my dad, and bring him with me.

With my dad in hand, I close the car door and head up the pathway leading to our new home. I don't look up the entire time, keeping my eyes lowered to just ahead of me. I refuse to give this woman the satisfaction of looking up to her as I ascend to my new home. Her home. I'm only a guest. This will never be my home.

This entire place is fucking weird. There's no other way to describe it.

"Come on child, I don't have all day," are the first words she utters. It startles me. My eyebrows raise to the sound of her voice. My blue eyes look up at her, the expression on her face remains unchanged, miserable and impatient. Her words tempt me to slow my pace even further. To see how far I can push her until she snaps. I've already disturbed her life simply by being here, and I doubt I'll find a welcome basket waiting for me in my room, if she's even given me a room. Maybe she will shove me in the basement or under the stairs in a closet.

Gripping my dad tighter, I need his strength to get through this. I feel his energy.

Fuck. I miss him.

Tears well in my eyes, but she doesn't get to see them. They're not for her. I keep my eyes open, refusing to blink, so the cool air dries them before they are able to stream down my cheek.

She can damn well wait the twenty seconds it takes for me to walk from my car to her.

Both of our faces are still stoic. Neither of us budging as I approach the stairs, and the space between us gets smaller. There are four wooden steps leading to the porch. I place one foot on the first step, and it creaks underneath my weight. Each step that follows creaks in succession.

I stop directly in front of Grandma Joanie and stare at her, expressionless. She smells like a mixture of woodsy pine and flowers, as if she spends a lot of time outside, although you could never tell by just looking at her. She's as pale as the rest of the towns-folk I saw when driving through. Surrounded by thick forests and mountains, the sun doesn't seem to shine much here. It's a little after 6pm and it's already starting to set, and autumn is just beginning.

We are still in a standoff.

Your move, bitch.

She still says nothing.

Instead, she clears her throat, turns around, opens one of the double doors and walks into the house.

Is this seriously happening?

I'm unable to hold my tongue. "The drive was fine, thank you. And thanks for coming to help when my dad died. You know, your son? No, no. I'll come back out and grab the rest. It's heavy and I would hate for you to strain yourself."

She stops in her tracks.

"Your room is upstairs. Hurry up. I have things to do."

It's her only response before proceeding up the staircase, leaving me standing on the porch.

I can't stay here.

Anxiety begins to fill my body.

Calling her was a horrible mistake.

I have to remember.

This is only temporary.

Once I figure my life out, I'll take my dad, and we can leave.

This is not permanent. I have to keep reminding myself of this. It's the only way I'll make it through.

Reluctantly, I follow Grandma Joanie inside. Stepping over the threshold, my eyes widen when I take in the interior of this massive old home. The inside is much the same as the outside, but not in a bad way. A giant staircase fashioned from black hardwood is crowned by the enormous windows behind it, while aged black-and-white tiles that have been polished to perfection lie beneath my feet. The walls are papered in royal purple and more black with more dark wood framing windows that allow for natural light to filter into the room. It must be stunning when the sun is shining.

The stairs part into opposite directions of the house at the top of the landing. Looking up, there is a large black chandelier hanging from the ceiling. It looks like it may have once held candle sticks which have since been replaced by lightbulbs.

On either side of the entrance are open archways leading to other parts of the house. Looking back towards the staircase, Grandma Joanie has gone left and is continuing to climb the stairs while holding onto the handrail. Not wanting to get lost, I stop taking in my new surroundings and reluctantly follow her.

A part of me can't wait to see this place in the daylight. It's incredible and not at all what I pictured when driving to Port Canyon.

Grandma Joanie is waiting on the second floor landing. Her back is turned to me, but she can hear my footsteps. Once I get close enough, she continues ahead. We proceed down the long hallway, past walls lined with the same dark wood with purple and black wallpaper. Black vintage candelabras illuminate the area, each holding four lit white candles. Wax drips down the stems, hardening along them. Unlike the tiled floor downstairs, this wing is carpeted in black with a creamy white border, the middle faded from what must be years of foot traffic.

Every part of me wants to hate this place, but it's absolutely stunning. I got to give it to the old bat, she has good taste.

We pass two closed doors and Grandma Joanie abruptly stops in front of a third.

"This is your room. I have two rules while you are here. No snooping and mind your business. Do you understand?" she questions. Not wanting to give her the satisfaction of getting to me, I reply with a simple, "Got it."

Grandma Joanie wastes no time leaving me on my own, walking past me back toward the staircase.

"Don't call me Grandma or Granny. You will address me as Joanie." I don't turn around. Only knowing she is gone when I hear her take each step back down to the main floor.

Fucking bitch. I refuse to let her get to me.

Grabbing the brass doorknob and turning it until I hear the click of the latch. The door creaks as I slowly open it. Gingerly stepping in with my dad still in hand, I find a room just as beautiful as the rest of the house.

Letting go of the door handle, I pat the wall for a light switch. Finding it easily, I flick it on, and the room lights up thanks to the glass ceiling light. The floors are a dark wood with a plush blood red carpet laying on top. A giant wooden bed with luxurious red and black bedding takes up most of the space. There is a closet off to the side, along with built-in shelving and a desk. The one window in the room looks out onto a space I don't yet recognize and thick velvet green curtains hang on either side. It's perfect.

Placing my dad on one of the shelves, I take it all in. I do not want to see that woman again today, ever actually, but what choice do I have? Instead of going back to my car for the rest of my things, I decide to close the door and hide in my new room for the rest of the night.

I'll face my new reality tomorrow. Tonight, I want to forget and pretend none of this was real.

CHAPTER 3
FALLON

I t's mid-day. After falling asleep last night, I'd expected to be awake often, but that didn't happen. This place is unknown to me and comfortable is not a word I would use to describe how I feel being here. By the time my body naturally woke up, it was already 11am.

It's been an exhausting couple of weeks, and this is the first time since my dad died that I've been able to sleep without my thoughts racing and keeping me awake. I'd been constantly running through a to-do list in my head, or feeling the pressure and anxiety of time running out before the bank locks the house doors on me. Last night, I put my head on the pillow and slept like the dead. And it was fucking amazing.

After getting dressed in a pair of black leggings, a white crop top hoodie, and my dirty, white high-top converse, I went to my car and got the rest of my stuff. All while successfully avoiding Joanie, who is not a grandmother, and I shall not dare mistake her as one. She is nothing more than my... landlord? No, because I don't pay rent. But maybe she'll drop that on me next.

For now, I guess we are roommates.

The crisp air fills my lungs with each breath. I close my eyes briefly, taking it all in for the first time as I wander the grounds outside. It's a beautiful fall day.

In California, we had fall, but nothing like this. Here, the leaves change colors, hundreds of shades of orange, red and yellow; falling off the trees and carpeting the forest floor below. There's a slight chill in the air. It's crisp, but not cold. Mountains and tall trees surround Port Canyon, and coming from the city, it's a nice change of scenery. I've never experienced anything like the absolute silence while standing outside.

The property is bigger than I had imagined. After coming out of the back door, and taking in my new home, my eyes were immediately drawn to a giant stone statue of an angel sitting with her hands resting atop a tall textured piece of wood. It kind of looks like it could be a torch. Her wings are stretched wide, and black tears stream down her face as she looks straight ahead. She's beautiful.

The statue stands in the middle of the backyard, surrounded by overgrown red and white rose bushes, and has to be at least ten or twelve feet tall. I wonder what she represents to this place.

Slowly making my way to her from the back porch, using the large stepping stones, I walk around her, taking in all the intricate details etched into the stone. Stepping closer, I see a small plaque at her feet which says:

'*Angel of Death*'

What an interesting piece to have in one's yard.

The entire backyard is surrounded by large green hedges. In one spot, is a curved archway made from a stone that matches the statue, moss and vines running along it. A thick black iron gate occupies the space in the middle. It has a large latch and handle and I can faintly see a stone path on the other side.

How big is this place?

Large trees peek over the hedges, and I wonder how deep in the path goes?

Where does it lead to?

Biting my lip, I remember Joanie's warning about not snooping and minding my own business.

Surely, she didn't mean out here. It's just a path.

Fuck it. I want to see what's back there if I am stuck living here.

CHAPTER 4

MERRICK

I watch Fallon from one of the second-floor windows as she slowly walks around the Angel of Death, noting how she takes in the perfect little flowers my charming mother, Joanie, tends to daily. This place is her fucking pride and joy. And that statue is this place's goddamn mascot. Not that Fallon would know that... yet.

The torch is upside down for a reason, representing a life extinguished. How fitting.

Right now, Fallon is taken in by its beauty and is naturally curious. I can tell by the way she is examining every inch of it.

Soon she will want to know more.

Ask more.

Soon she will see it's too fucking late.

The statue symbolizes everything I tried to run from. The burden it has placed on this family.

Unless you're my mother, then it is a gift and a privilege.

That night, I thought I had escaped.

I should have known better. This place always sucks you back in. It will always have a hold over you. Coming here will be Fallon's biggest mistake, and I will make sure she knows it. I will make sure she regrets her decision to call my cold-hearted mother. If Fallon tries to run, it will be because I am the one chasing her.

To see the look on her face when she realizes she can't leave will be goddamn perfection.

Some may think I'm jaded.

I couldn't give a fuck. She shouldn't have come here. She shouldn't have called my fucking mother to save her. No one can save her.

The Angel of Death is only the half of it.

Stupid, stupid girl.

There are secrets beyond the perfectly trimmed hedges and iron gates, you have to see to believe.

Raking my hand through my white blond hair, I take another hit off my joint.

My poor brother even got sucked back in after leaving Port Canyon over thirty years ago.

Blowing out the smoke from between my lips, and putting the joint out on the wood frame of the window, I look back down at Fallon, who is now walking toward the iron gate.

She looks just fucking like him.

CHAPTER 5
FALLON

A shiver runs down my spine when my hand grabs hold of the cold iron handle and my thumb presses down on the lever. The gate gives and the release of the latch is audible in the silence of the backyard. Before opening it fully, I turn around and look up at the house to make sure Joanie isn't watching. Examining all floors and trying to see through all the windows, I can't see her glaring down at me in what I assume would be disapproval, so I proceed.

Pushing forward, the hinges squeak when I open the gate and my heart races. If she hears me, she will stop me. Knowing I need to move faster, I open it enough for my body to slip through, then once on the other side, I grab hold of a bar and close it behind me.

Taking one last look back at the house, still seeing no sign of her, I turn around and start my way down the weathered stone path. It feels colder on this side of the gate.

Large trees with thick branches hang over me, blocking out the sunlight and lining the path as far as the eye can see. Blowing out a breath, I can faintly see the condensation linger briefly, before finally evaporating into the air.

Looking around, there's nothing that immediately catches my eye.

My feet take me further in.

Wild flowers appear alongside the long wild grass, taking up any space where the thick tree trunks aren't. The loud caws of crows startle me. Looking overhead, I can't see them, but the branches are rustling. I'm unsure of how many are watching me, but I don't let it deter my curiosity. What else is down here?

Ahead there is another stone archway, this time without a gate, and it leads into another open space. There's something else in the distance. It's tall, possibly another statue like the one from the backyard.

Quickening my pace, the crows continue to squawk above me. A couple decide to fly above me, but I'm unbothered by their presence. I want to see what my new home has to offer. Rushing through the arch, the stone path stops and what I see before me is shocking.

Absolutely unexpected.

There is another statue. Only this time, the angel's wings are closed, and he is down on bent knees with both hands, palms up, facing the sky. He has long hair and a floral headpiece. This statue is surrounded by lilies and chrysanthemums.

On either side of me, rows upon rows of head-stones fill the area. Some are tall with crosses or angels, others are shorter with pieces missing, either chipped or have fallen off. All appear to be made of cement or stone. Further ahead is a huge mausoleum, it sits under a pair of large trees. The peaked roof is weathered with age and overgrown with moss. Intricate designs of angels, skulls, flowers and filigree decorate the space between the door and the top of it.

Shocked by what is in front of me, I haven't moved. My eyes are still taking everything in as my brain tries to digest what it's seeing.

This graveyard goes on for acres, easily.

Where the fuck am I?

Before I'm able to make my way further in, a girl, maybe my age, jumps out from behind the statue. She seems overly bubbly and smiles with wide eyes. She seems out of place here with her long black hair, baggy black hoodie, boyfriend jeans and black converse shoes.

"You must be the new girl. I'm Harper." She spits out at me rapidly.

There is too much going on in my head right now. This person is the last thing I need.. I don't do people and based on Joanie's reaction to me, they don't do me either. Except I already knew that. My father's charismatic charm got lost in my DNA. I tolerate people and they tolerate me.

Not having replied, she tries talking to me again. "So, how are you liking it here? You're probably wondering why I'm in your yard? I live across the street from the graveyard with my dad. He's the town's mortician, and he's started training me to take over. I find it peaceful here during the day."

I survey her again, not quite sure what to make of her and this new information yet.

"I see you're not up for visitors today. Still adjusting. That's ok, really. I'll come by tomorrow and maybe we can hang out? You're the first new person here in over fifty years and the fact that you're the next in line to protect and care for the graveyard and its guests is perfect!" She says, spreading her arms wide, then continues, "We will be best friends, you'll see. Our fate was written before we were even born. Did you know that? This was meant to happen."

Is she high? What in the fuck is she going on about?

Harper, I think that's her name, starts walking off into the thick tree line. But before fully disappearing into it, she turns around, "It's ok, Fallon. Just breathe and I'll be back tomorrow." And then, that's it. She's gone.

My knees buckle. My brain feels dizzy as I fall to the hard ground beneath me.

My mind is firing off questions in quick succession that I don't have the answers to.

What did she mean it's peaceful during the day? What happens at night? And guests? Does Joanie host tours here or some shit? What fucking legacy or generational inheritance bullshit have I walked into? There was nothing in dad's will explaining Joanie's property as his inheritance, so why does Harper think it's mine to take?

Yet the biggest and most important question is clear and unanswered: What the actual fuck is this place and how soon can I get the hell out of here?

Closing my eyes, I take a couple of deep breaths in and out. My heart rate slows from the insanely fast pace it was at from moments ago. Opening my eyes, I look around the well-manicured graveyard once more. A cool breeze blows past me.

Harper was right. This place is peaceful. But peace won't give me the answers I need.

I'm coming back here tonight.

CHAPTER 6
FALLON

The sun has set.

The night sky has arrived.

Anxiety thrums through my body in anticipation.

After the minor stroke I suffered in the graveyard, thanks to the bombs of encrypted information Harper dropped on me, I snuck back to the house.

I had to be sure that Joanie didn't catch me. If she had, there would have been no chance of me sneaking back out there this evening. Once I made it back into the yard, I scanned the windows, not seeing any sign of her.

Rushing into the house, I made my way to the main grand staircase. Before making it up safely,

Joanie walked out of the library at the front of the house.

"Dinner is in ten minutes. Wash up. Don't be late." Is all she said to me as we crossed paths.

Miserable bitch. She will get hers one day.

Dinner was uneventful. We sat in silence in the dining room, on opposite ends of the longest dark wood table I have ever seen. A deep purple tablecloth ran the length of it, lined with unlit candles and surrounded by tall, dark chairs. Just like the main entrance, a chandelier hung from above. Joanie made us roast and potatoes, though I'm sure she put something in my portion. Probably trying to kill me with rat poison, so it looks like a natural death. I'm on to you, Joanie. Two can play that game. Don't try me, bitch.

I don't have any evidence of this, but I wouldn't put it past the old broad.

After excusing myself, I went back up to my room where I am now, waiting for the right moment to go back outside.

The small lamp on my bedside table is on while I lay here in bed, staring at the ceiling, waiting for Joanie to go to sleep. Her room isn't in this wing.

That much has been made obvious to me. No hearing the door shut or her footsteps walking past the door to give me a hint on how much longer I must wait.

Maybe I'll make that a mission for tomorrow, but in the meantime, it's a guessing game I hope to win.

Checking my phone, it's been hours of mindless scrolling, and it's already after midnight.

Fuck it. I'm going. There's no way she's still up.

Sitting up against my pillows, I begin to move to the edge of the bed when a cold chill moves across my body. It's not cold in the room and I'm in a black hoodie with matching leggings and black converse.

It doesn't make sense. Unless it's just this drafty old house.

Just as I am about to stand from the edge of the bed, my breath is stolen from me. It feels like something is wrapping itself around my throat, squeezing it tightly. I try to gasp for air, but instead, all I can do is cough, hoping even the tiniest amount of air is able to slip by to help me. My hands reach up, trying to grab at whatever it is restricting me, but nothing is there.

Then, as suddenly as it began, my body is thrown back to the bed where it bounces on the mattress. Tears fill my eyes as I gasp for air. The tightness is gone. My chest is heaving and I'm rubbing my neck, trying to make the feeling of phantom hands disappear.

Before I am able to comprehend what just occurred, my hands are thrown to either side of me and the tightness is back.

This time, my body is lifted off the bed. The pressure is too much. I bring my hands back up to my throat, desperately trying to fight off whatever is doing this to me. My legs swing in the air, trying to stop whatever is happening.

Nothing is working.

I try to gasp for another breath that I will never get, and my body slams violently against the wall. My head bounces off of it, and the lamp and bed frame shake from the impact.

Gasping for air—I'll take anything—my lungs are contracting and panic is setting in. I'm going to die here.

My eyes feel like they are about to bulge out of my head, and then I feel a sharp sting along my cheek and my head whips to the side from the force.

My hands are still struggling with whatever has me pinned like this. How do I get out of this?

As my hope fades, my coughs become fewer and my lungs continue to beg me to breathe, a deep voice, nothing more than a whisper, speaks next to my ear.

"Stupid fucking girl. You have no idea what you've done."

My body goes rigid once the threat settles in.

This is it.

Yet, my life isn't flashing before me. Instead, all I feel is my racing heart deep within my chest. Why do people lie about what happens before they think it's all over? I see no memories of my childhood, no reassuring words from my dad saying '*it's going to be ok*', these fucking liars.

My chest contracts again, desperately looking for air, and I begin to accept this is my end. The sting of my cheek, nothing more than a memory.

Closing my eyes in preparation, I think it will hurt less if my eyes are closed, whatever it is.

Then, my body falls. Slamming on top of the bed. I cough as air reenters my lungs. Tears are streaming down my face. My body trembles with the shock.

I don't feel scared, but I also don't feel right.

I'm so fucking confused.

Bringing my knees up to my chest, holding them close, my brain is desperately racing to catch up with what just occurred.

At this moment, I feel alone.

Daddy, why did you leave me?

CHAPTER 7
MERRICK

*D*addy, *I miss you. Daddy, I need you. Please come back. Why did you leave me?*

Once the pity party started, I got out of there. The poor me princess bullshit is pathetic. No one is coming to save you. And you're not going anywhere.

But fuck, will I have fun trying to push you to run, only to see your face when you realize you're fucking stuck here. Just like the rest of us.

She had choices. She didn't need to come. She could have gone anywhere else.

What a fucking waste.

I'm back in my room. I don't socialize.

You wouldn't catch me dead or alive in that fucking graveyard with the rest of them.

Sucking back on another joint, my head resting against the wall as I'm sitting on the floor under the windowsill.

All I can think about is what else I'm going to do to that stupid little girl.

The rush when my hand wrapped tightly around her tiny neck was incredible. The crack of her skin when I slapped it, and how her body flung around like a rag doll as I pinned her against the wall was exhilarating. The power is remarkable.

Her pain gives me pleasure. It's the first thing I've felt in a long fucking time.

CHAPTER 8
FALLON

Exhausted. Confused. And freaked the fuck out, would describe my mental state this morning. My body aches.. I cried until no more tears could come out of me. Eventually falling asleep, while still cradling myself on my bed where it left me. Whatever 'it' is. I have no fucking idea.

I do know it was real.

I felt it. I still feel where it squeezed my neck. My face throbbed from where I was slapped. My head aches from where it hit the wall. It wasn't a hallucination, it was fucking real. None of this would have happened if my dad was still here. Why did he have to die? He left me. Here. In this creepy fucking house with his evil mother. If he would have stayed alive, this wouldn't be happening. I wouldn't have had to call her. I have never felt as alone as I do now. Joanie would hate me even more than she already does if I were to tell her what happened, and surely she would not believe me. There is no one I can tell.

Pull yourself together, Fallon. Goddammit. You are stronger than this. Self pity is not a good look on anyone. I allow myself one more minute in this state. Stretching my body out, rubbing my bloodshot and swollen eyes, I tell myself I will not let this place win. After blowing out one final breath, I swing my legs out over the bed. The last time I did this, I was assaulted. My heart races, waiting for it to happen again. It's quiet. Sun is peeking through the curtains. Grabbing my phone from my pocket, it's already past noon. Shit.

Standing, my legs shake for a moment. I reach the bed for support while my body catches up with my brain. Once my legs have settled, I walk to my closed bedroom door and open it, peering out into the hall. It is still quiet, no sign of life within the hall. The bathroom is next door to my room. Making my way to it, the floor creaks beneath me. As I enter the bathroom and flick the light on, I am captivated by one of the large bay windows at the front of the house. Each frame is lined with dark black wood, and there is a ledge running alongside one, where white and black candles sit, waiting to be lit. Most sit directly on the wooden ledge, but a few are in these incredible holders, with melted wax dried down them. A few green plants hang over the ledge of the other windows in the room. There's a dark purple velvet chair sitting next to the black and gold standalone clawfoot tub tucked into the nook under a window.

The floor is black marble with gray veins running through it. It looks like one solid piece. The walls are painted black, with a filigree pattern on them. The same as what is on the mausoleum in the graveyard. Walking to the black basin sink that sits atop the counter, I turn the gold faucet and hold my hands beneath as cold water pools in them. Splashing my face with it several times, forcing my body to wake up and join the rest of me.

I grab the towel hanging from the ring and pat myself dry. I'd avoided the mirror since walking in, but screw it, let's see the damage. Moving the towel off my face, I look up and see my reflection. My eyes are swollen, as I had already suspected. One cheek is red, but it's not very noticeable unless you are looking for it. Dropping the towel onto the counter, my neck is exposed. It's bruised already, and it is noticeably a handprint. Turning my head, I can see the thumbprint on one side and the ridged tips of fingers along with a palm print surrounding the rest. Subconsciously, I find myself tracing along it with my fingers. Enamored by it.

How is this possible?

Oddly enough, I kind of like it. The coloring, mottled purples and blues with a hint of redness. It's satisfying against my pale skin. A wave of exhaustion washes over me. I am mentally and physically exhausted. But at the same time, I'm curious. The need to know more has heightened since last night. I leave the bathroom and race back to my room. The door is closed, though I don't remember closing it. Strange. Maybe Joanie came by?

I am in a state of disbelief when I open the door. What little I had is scattered across the floor. Dresser drawers included. Why would she do this?

The only thing untouched is my dad's ashes. They are still right where I left them.

This bitch has lost her fucking mind if she thinks I'm going to sit quietly and take this. She has no idea what my last twenty-four hours have been like. Today is not the day to test me.

Too pissed off to clean up, I quickly find an over-sized hoodie to swap out with the one I'm wearing. This one has more give and will cover my neck to avoid any questioning. Once changed, I rush out of my room, slamming the door in hopes she hears it. Not wanting to give her the satisfaction of rushing to her and confronting her, I pace myself walking down the stairs.

Once in the main entrance, I walk to the kitchen first, but she isn't there. Then the TV room, study and finally the library. Still no sign of her. There's no way she moved through this giant house this quickly. Frustrated, I go outside, hoping the fresh air will clear my head. The cool air against my skin feels nice. I walk briskly past the angel statue on my way to the gate. Maybe the graveyard will offer the silence I need to think. Taking the long path under the trees, I stop before opening it.

She's out here. But how?

Joanie is bent over trimming the flowers around the kneeled statue, murmuring to herself, but it's nothing I can make out clearly. Standing motionless, I continue to watch her as she makes her way to the mausoleum to tidy the vines up. As she finishes, she says, "Y'all are ungrateful. I keep this place tidy for you. Keep you from outsiders. The least you can do is show your faces and thank me!"

Who is she talking to?

"She does this every day." A voice whispers in my

ear. It startles me, but I'm careful not to make a noise. Turning around, I see it's Harper.

"You scared the shit out of me!" I hiss back at her, and she mouths *'sorry'*. I grab her arm and drag her into the thick tree line. She clearly has answers to my questions and she will give them to me. We are a couple of feet in when I let go of her. "Explain. What do you mean she does this every day? Does what? Who is she talking to?"

Harper just looks at me. I can tell by the look in her eyes that she's thinking about how much she wants to tell me.

Finally speaking up, "You honestly have no idea?" she questions. Obviously not. Fuck. Who is this chick?

"No idea about what?"

Harper's eyebrows scrunch. Her face goes from amused, to thinking, to confused, all in a matter of seconds. She slowly shakes her head in disbelief. "I shouldn't. I can't. You need to talk to Joanie." Harper's eyes squint as she takes me in. "Fallon, you look like shit. Are you ok?"

Now is not the time.

"No. I'm not ok. My night… My night was completely fucked up. I was attacked. My room was trashed. I'm fucking exhausted. And now you won't tell me what is going on here? Where am I?"

Harper is taken aback by my words, even taking a step away from me.

"Who attacked you? Did Joanie do something to you, Fallon?" She questions. I'm quick to respond, "No. She didn't do this to me. She did trash my room. I have no idea who choked me out and threw me against the wall. So, tell me something. Anything. Please." I beg.

She takes a deep breath in. Her mind is racing.

"It can't be, can it? I wonder. No." She's mumbling under her breath.

"What can't be?" I snap back.

"I should go. But you really should try talking to Joanie. And soon. I don't think she's the one that trashed your room either. Come find me after you talk to her. But I don't feel right saying anything until you do, Fallon." With that, Harper walks off in the direction we came in from, leaving me alone. A cool breeze passes by me, and my skin chills.

I'm not talking to that old bitch. There must be answers around here somewhere.

CHAPTER 9
FALLON

The more I search, the more questions appear with no answers to follow. After Harper left me, I came back to the house, deciding to leave Joanie to whatever the fuck it is she was doing. My brain is begging me to leave. My gut is telling me this is where I need to be. I need answers. No matter what is trying to push me out or who.

My dad always said trust your gut, so I am. Nothing will get in my way.

I'm freshly showered. The redness on my cheek has faded. While the bruise on my neck is more vibrant, and my headache is almost gone. Wrapped in my towel, I walk back to my room. It's still a mess, but it's a mess I'll take care of tomorrow.

Then, out of nowhere, my spine shivers, causing the hairs on my arms to rise and goosebumps cover my body. It's the same cool breeze washing over me that I've felt over the past couple of days. My heart begins to race. It's going to happen again. I just know it. Bracing myself, I wait. But nothing happens.

Looking around, I lower my guard. I'm not a paranoid person and I refuse to let this place make me one. Then something catches my attention in my peripheral vision.

Refusing to look, "Who. Are. You?" Is all I can think of to say. But the room remains quiet. It wants me to see it.

Quickly, I turn around, hoping to catch it off guard, but nothing is there. What the… I swear I saw something. Turning back around, I do not expect to see what I do. Within an inch of my face, there is a man staring down at me. My mouth opens in fear, but nothing comes out.

His skin is more pale than mine. He has thick dark eyebrows and messy white blonde hair hanging over his forehead. Cold blue eyes stare down at me. He has no visible facial hair, and his thin lips are expression-less. Scanning down the length of his body, he has to be at least 6 feet tall. His frame filling a black tee, distressed black skinny jeans and worn combat boots. A couple of thin bracelets line his wrist and he stinks of weed. He isn't thin, but isn't built either. His fingernails have chipped black polish on them.

Moving my eyes back up his body, I realize he is so close to me I should be able to feel his breath invading my space. Watching his chest, it doesn't move. Not even once. My eyes widen, as I meet his. He tilts his head slightly, and I'm not sure what to expect next. He stands like this for a few moments, while neither of us speaks or moves. I don't think I could move even if I wanted to.

Before I am even able to register what is happening, my body is spun around so my back is to him. His cold hands grip my wrists, and he holds them behind me. Once he has them gripped in one hand, I hear the sound of his zipper lowering.

"No, no, no. Please don't do this." I plead as tears well in my eyes.

There's nothing but silence behind me. Instead, he pushes me forward so I am bent at the waist and my chest is against the mattress. The towel is moved up past my waist and then I feel the pressure of his free hand holding my head down. He kicks my legs apart with his leather boots, and it stings against my skin.

Then, without warning, he thrusts into me. Showing no restraint. His movements are fast and hard. The sound of our skin slapping against each other echoes around the room. I haven't had sex in almost a year. The intrusion of his cock hurts, my body wasn't given any time to adjust to his size. He has to notice how tight I am, but he doesn't care.

Tears silently run down my cheeks. I focus on one spot on the wall and start to zone out. My body isn't responding, but that doesn't stop him as he continues to work himself inside of me repeatedly. Just as I begin to hope it will end soon, he grunts and whispers, "Fuck," into the room. I feel his release coating my walls. Warm cum fills me as he works himself through his orgasm. His thrusts begin to slow, and he lets go of my head as he thrusts one final time inside me. Pulling out, I can feel his cum dripping out of me and the sound of his zipper being pulled up fills the silent room. He pulls me up by my wrists, which he still has a hold on, and brings his lips up to my ear; his touch is cold as he brushes his lips alongside the outside of my ear. He nips on my lobe, then whispers, "You shouldn't have come here. Stupid little girl. I'm going to fucking destroy you."

"I'll leave," is my response. It is the only thing I

can think of which will make this stop. Instead, it only encourages a laugh out of him.

"I'd like to see you try."

Then he's gone. His cold touch on my wrist is nothing more than phantom. The pressure of his body against mine disappears. I begin to shake, and I'm sure it's in shock like it was last night. Then something clicks in my head. There was something very familiar about him. I've seen him before. Rushing over to the shelves, I grab my photo album that is still on the floor and begin flipping the pages. I know it's in here. My towel falls to the ground, but I don't care. What more could happen to me that hasn't already? That's when I see it. Stopping on the page where my dad is in his graduation gown in Port Canyon's town center. Next to him is his big brother. His big brother died over thirty years ago after driving his car off the town's only bridge in or out.

How is this real life? This is something you only see on TV. The person that just force fucked me, is my uncle.

That was Merrick!

Rubbing my bruised neck, I wonder, was this him too? But how?

Why is this fucking town so weird? My dad never

talked about his place, said it was better forgotten than remembered. This place was my last resort. Shit.

Fuck your threats, Merrick.

He is just as miserable as Joanie. Neither of them will win.

I am not leaving Port Canyon until I get some fucking answers.

CHAPTER 10
MERRICK

Fallon's pussy was as dry as the fucking desert. I haven't fucked in thirty years and that was my grand return to it.

Disappointing. And Quick.

Don't get it twisted, I've jerked off over the years. My efforts were not short-lived because my balls were backlogged. It was because her pussy was as tight as the noose that this town has wrapped around my neck.

I guess the secret is out. I'm a fucking ghost. Boo! Are you scared yet?

I know what you're thinking. How can a ghost fuck? Where do you think American Horror got the idea to portray ghosts the way they do? From real ghosts. Obviously. We aren't that cartoony shit you see on TV, no white sheets here.

Joanie has a television room and once she's all tucked away in her wing sleeping, I'll pop it on. I know all about ghosts on TV.

Anyway, back to how we aren't cartoon characters.

Ghosts are here, in the same form as the moment of our last breath. We decide when you see us, and when you don't.

This place is in a graveyard, so of course there are more of us.

I don't hang out with the others, though. I'm a loner and have a fucking house. There is no need for me to be out in the yard with the others. I only leave to meet my dealer for weed each week. He hasn't even seen me. One day, I left a note for him with cash, and the next day the baggie of weed was hidden in the agreed-upon spot. I stayed hidden, so even if he was lurking, he wouldn't see who I was. We've continued this over the years, and now his kid is now learning the trade.

I'm not sure if you've heard, but this place passes its responsibilities down from generation to generation. My dealer's family's role is the illegal drug trade that fuels half of this town. Each founding family has a legacy to uphold, and sometimes the next generation wants nothing to do with it, like me. It consumes you.

Others love it, and pride themselves in learning the trade. Pathetic, really.

Regardless, the residents are bound here. I call it a curse.

Look at what happened to my brother. The town made him think he was safe. That he was the one to get out. Now he's dead and his daughter has taken his place.

I'm back in my room now. Smoking a joint, sitting on my bed and staring at the ceiling. I feel no remorse about what I did earlier. Call me evil, call me a terrible person, and then ask me if I care. The answer would be no.

I guess, technically, she is my niece, my family. I suppose I should be warm and welcoming, like Joanie. Fuck, my mom has not changed since the day I drove myself off that bridge. Whatever.

I can't be bothered to want to protect her from the inevitable. She dug her grave, and she can fucking lay in it. Coming here will always be her biggest regret. Just wait. You will see, she will hate it.

Trapped.

No way out.

Held back by your legacy.

Port Canyon does get tourists, but only during October, for Halloween. People have heard about this place, the rumors and folktales intrigue the visitors. The town puts on a show for them, and it fulfills their curiosity until the next year.

I never participated when I was alive. However, I would go into the town square looking for pussy. Whispering promises I would protect them from the monsters. They would melt in my hands and believe the bullshit I was spewing. Let's be real though, if a monster did come for us, I would leave whatever bitch I was banging and get the fuck out of there. They meant nothing to me other than being a mediocre fuck. A different variety of pussy for one month a year. No point in reminiscing about that now. It was over 30 years ago.

Plus, I am one now, aren't I? A monster. A scary ghost.

So now you know my story. Sort of. Well, as much as I want you to know.

Now fuck off. I'm sure Fallon's treasure hunt can keep you entertained.

CHAPTER II
FALLON

I've continued to avoid Joanie like the plague. Harper told me to talk to her, ask her questions, but she doesn't see the Joanie I do. This bitch wouldn't tell me shit if I had a gun pointed at her head. We avoid each other. Since that one night we had dinner together, we fend for ourselves. I think we both prefer it this way.

I'm in the library, which is hauntingly beautiful like the rest of the house. There are plush emerald green couches, and decorative chairs with white throw blankets hanging over them, silently inviting you to sit and curl up with a good book chosen from the massive shelves that line the walls. On any other day, I would. The many windows light up the space as I'm rummaging around, looking for answers to what is happening. I've noticed Joanie spends a good amount of time here when she isn't outside or in her wing of the house. Who knows what she does over there. I don't need or want to picture it. Right now, I am on a mission.

What is this place? How does what Joanie does in the graveyard tie back me? And why can't fucking Harper just tell me?

Screw it not being her place. My entire attitude has changed after being here for a few days. I've gone from grieving daughter to confused and alone, to being assaulted and dicked by my dead uncle, who didn't seem fully dead when his dick was inside of me.

Now I'm on a mission, and no one is getting in my way. A fire has been lit. Once I start getting some answers, Harper better fill in the goddamn blanks. I will invoke the best friend card. If she wants to act like we are destined, then she better start acting like it.

As soon as I got in here, I scanned the book-shelves and began pulling whatever looked to be the oldest. What I need are origin stories. Family history. Anything that will help me understand this situation.

None of these older books have titles on the spines, so I don't know what I am grabbing until it's in my hands. Some titles are simply boring, herbology nonsense. Others, I can't be sure what they mean. When I flip the pages, it's in a completely different language, which is no help at all. I'm about to throw another useless one to the side when a sound comes from above me. "This is the one you're looking for, stupid little girl."

Merrick is standing in the air, like it's completely normal, and holding a book in his hand.

He can never know I'm secretly seriously impressed.

"Well, can you pass it to me, then?" I respond impatiently.

"Tsk, tsk. Where are your manners?"

He is enjoying this way too much, asshole.

I comply just to get him to go away. "Please, uncle dearest, may you pass that very informative book to me?" Finishing it with a smile.

His face doesn't change from its cold expression when I drop the uncle bomb. That's right, Merrick. This stupid little girl knows.

I can't be more of a smartass out loud to him when he is holding what I need, though. Bastard.

A few moments pass before he moves, and he's a complete dick head. Why can't he be a decent dead person? He opens the hand the book is in and simply lets it drop. It's like watching it in slow motion as I dive for it. The thing looks like it's from the dawn of time. If it smashes into the hardwood floor, there is no telling what could happen. Break? Maybe turn into dust. It's not worth the risk to not have to watch it fall to its death.

The pages are flapping on their descent; they look stained and extremely delicate. The binding is the same aged leather as the others with the curved spine. My efforts aren't wasted and as it lands in my hand seconds before hitting the floor, I blow out a sigh of relief. Tilting my head up, I see he's already gone.

Which is fine. He served his purpose.

Moving to the couch, I place the book in my lap. This is it. This is what is going to tell me everything I need to know about this creepy fucking town. Why my dad left and never returned. Why his brother drove off a bridge and why Harper wants me to talk to Joanie so badly about this property.

Rubbing my fingers over the stamped leather letters that spell the name of this miserable town, I summon the courage to open it. Ok, Port Canyon, show me what you got.

I flip the thick cover open and see everything is in handwritten ink. The pages feel like aged parchment. This book has to be at least a hundred years old.

The first line tells me it's much older than I thought,

Port Canyon was founded in 1833 by a group of families who wanted to build their own society far away from others. They settled deep within the mountains and forests of Washington State, where no other colonizers could stumble upon them by accident. It took thirteen days for them to chop enough lumber to construct a bridge, then an additional thirty-one days to build it. The bridge is the only way in and out of Port Canyon.

The founding families cast a hex over Port Canyon for protection.

Instilling fear and ensuring unwanted guests would never make it to the end of the bridge.

Legend says it was the town that kept them out. No bodies would ever be found on the bridge. That the town would take them.

Outsiders would only interfere with their generational teachings.

These families valued their way of thinking. They valued their legacies.

Each role in the community was sacred to their individual bloodline. Only blood could take over from blood, inheriting the jobs from their elders. Once it was time for the torch to be passed down, a ceremony would take place. During the rise of the full moon, the next generation would have. to draw enough blood from their elders to fill the silver goblet.

Blood for blood.

Every last drop of blood would be drunk by the next generation. Once the ceremony is complete, according to the legend, the legacy would be officially passed down. Although, if someone outside of the bloodline tried to drink the blood, the blood would know and kill them slowly and painfully.

If anyone from the families tried to abandon their responsibilities, the town would curse them. Some say they were riddled with disease if they disobeyed. Others say the town would let them escape, make them feel like they got away with it, then curse their children.

Bringing them back to uphold the bloodline.

The Founding Families
  Hayes - Mortician
  Wade - Medicine
  Rainford - Healers
  Marwood - Butchers

Harvey - Blacksmiths
Gladstone - Builders
Knight - Grave keepers

I stop reading as soon as I see my last name.

Knight. We are a founding family. Grave keepers.

My dad left. My dad died. This was my only option after it happened. The town took me back.

Flipping the page, I continue.

As time went on and the first elder passed away from natural causes. The Hayes family prepared the body and the Knight family completed the burial.

Then, after the first new moon, the elder reappeared. He was in the same form in which he died. Although he was still dead. He was pale, cold to the touch, and was able to appear and disappear as he pleased in his spirit form. The elder explored, able to leave the graveyard at night, but bound to it by day. The Knight family then became the keepers of the dead. The Hayes family always ensured they prepared the body as the living requested before their death.

The town never lets its people leave.

As the years went on, tales began to spread about

what happened across the bridge in Port Canyon. Curious eyes wanted to see the mystery for themselves.

Once a year, during the month of October, the town opens itself up to visitors, and at11:59pm on Halloween night, the town closes itself off again.

My dad left with my mom in October. She came here as a visitor. He was captivated by her and decided to go back to California with her. My mom fucked off after I was born, leaving only my dad and me.

He died suddenly. Was that the curse?

Fuck.

I'm the last one left.

The town brought me back here to fulfill my duties.

CHAPTER 12

FALLON

After letting myself digest what I just read. I cleaned up the library, putting all the books back where I found them. Of course, this one was on the top shelf, so I stacked a couple of the chairs onto the coffee table I moved, and stuck it back from where Merrick dropped it from.

Asshole couldn't come back and help, could he?

Before I confront Joanie, I need to talk to Harper.

Rushing out the front door, I hurry down the long driveway, passing my beautiful car. The same car that brought me here, and transported my dad back to Port Canyon with memories of his deceased older brother. Harper was right—our fate has already been written. And I had no idea I was driving right towards it.

The gate is huge and closed until I activate the sensors to open it on my approach. The moment there is enough room for me to pass through, I do and run across to Harper's house, which thankfully isn't as deep into the property as Joanie's.

Walking up the front porch stairs, I'm about to knock on the door, but it opens first.

"It's about time," Harper says, like she already knows why I'm here. "So you talked to Joanie?"

Shaking my head, "No, I found a book in her library."

"Dad, I'll be back. I'm going out with Fallon."

A deep voice shouts back, "Ok, baby. I love you."

"Love you too," she shouts back while closing the door.

"Where are we going? I have a million questions rushing through my head." I question her.

"Let's go to the cemetery. It will be easier to explain. It's after three, so Joanie should be heading back to the house by now." I don't question how she knows this. At this point, I really don't care. I need to know if what I read is true.

We walk in silence across the street, up the long driveway and through the backyard to the graveyard. Looking around the area, there is no sign of Joanie anywhere. Harper was right, she's gone for the day. I follow Harper as she takes the lead through the archway and leads us to a spot under one of the large trees next to a few tombstones. We both sit, leaning against the tree. She clearly has something to share, and I wait for her to begin.

"By now, you know it's not an accident you're here. This is our fate, it has always been written for us. Our legacy is our responsibility. We are the town's bloodline. My dad is training me to take his spot as the mortician. In the next couple of years, he will pass the torch onto me and one day, I will pass it on to my kin." Harper pauses to let me process. Seeing that I am still confused, she gestures to the graveyard around us and continues.

"Your family is responsible for this place, including the spirits that call it home. There are hundreds of years of history here. Most spirits will come out once they feel comfortable with you. Some you will never see; they are too shy or prefer to keep to themselves. It is your job to keep them safe. To keep them happy and to help them transition into the afterlife. This is their home as much as it is yours. My family prepares them so your family can place them in their final resting spot. Your family helps them adjust and takes care of them. The Angel of Death in your backyard represents the extinguishing of a life. It was the original symbol for your family. The Angel of Mercy was added later, and she represents mercy for the dead who reside here. Show them mercy in the afterlife and in their spirit form." She says all of this while looking forward, not turning her head to face me until now.

"You said something the other day that makes me wonder. You said you were assaulted, but not by Joanie. The spirits here wouldn't ever violate some-one's privacy without consent. Going into the main house is strictly off limits. And Joanie can be very private. So, I guess what I'm trying to ask is... Did you see Merrick?" I look back at Harper, and she appears nervous. Almost scared of what I might say, but there is no point beating around it.

"Yes."

Harper looks down, and I can tell her mind is racing. "No one has seen him since the night he died. He has never shown himself or even made himself known. Fallon! This is major! We don't think he's even appeared for his mom."

"The guy is a total asshole. He choked me. Threw me against a wall and slapped my face. I'm pretty sure he wants me gone. Which makes no sense, if he knows I can't leave. He must know that, right?" I intentionally leave out the part where he fucked me. She is still processing the fact that I saw him, there's no need to drop another bomb on her. Even though I have had several dropped on me today.

She doesn't respond, so I continue.

"You know, Joanie hasn't exactly been a ball of warmth. Actually, she's been a complete bitch to me since I arrived. I don't understand. If I am her legacy, wouldn't she be excited that I'm here?"

Harper turns her head, resting it on the trunk of the tree tilted toward the sky.

"I've heard talk, rumors, really. That Joanie became obsessed with her duties. They say that's why Merrick drove off the bridge. Then your dad left, and she only became more invested in it and got more protective. It's not my story to tell, but even the spirits have seen a shift in her over the years." She sounds apprehensive, but carries on. "You should hang out here more. Let them get used to you. Maybe they will become comfortable enough to show themselves to you. Then they can explain more to you, or at least more than I can. As for Merrick, if he is showing himself to you, there is a reason behind it. I'm telling you, no one has seen him."

Shaking my head, "Harper, I need you to focus.

You're skipping the most important part. I am stuck here. I didn't even get a choice and now I'm supposed to become the keeper of all of this? Which I know nothing about, and Joanie isn't exactly a willing teacher." Fuck me, what am I saying? Why do I care that she isn't a willing teacher? I can't do this.

"Just spend some time here. The spirits will help you if you let them, but you have to let them in. You have to get to know them and vice versa." Is all she says.

I can tell her intentions are pure, but dammit, it is pissing me off. I want to know everything now. I need to know more about what the fuck I have walked into.

Blowing out a breath, and still shaking my head, I sigh. "Fine. I can do that."

This brings a smile to her face. "Good. The Grave keeper and the Mortician. I told you we were meant to be best friends. You will see!"

I laugh at her. Mostly from her excitement, the rest is because that is all I can do. Otherwise, I may start crying, and we decided we aren't doing that anymore. I am on a mission and I will not rest until I figure it all out.

"I'm going to go so you can start spending time with them, alone. If you need anything, I'm across the street. Even if you don't need anything, you can still stop by, maybe?"

I can tell she must not have many friends, though her quirkiness is growing on me. "I will. Thank you, Harper." I say as she stands up. She doesn't respond, and walks off in the same direction we came.

Ok, let's spend time with some ghosts.

CHAPTER 13
MERRICK

S o she thinks I'm a *total asshole*. How juvenile.

"Merrick, I know you're up there! I felt you going in front of me earlier," Fallon shouts while still sitting at the bottom of the tree. Only because I wanted you to know, stupid little girl.

I've been hanging around since I died and Joanie still doesn't have a fucking clue.

Making myself appear on the thick tree branch above, I announce myself.

"Yes, the total asshole is indeed up here." I don't give a fuck and it's clear in my tone.

She lets out a sigh in response and I can almost guarantee she rolled her eyes. She will be punished for that later. Pathetically, she asks, "Why me?"

"I'm not your fucking therapist."

"Jesus Christ, Merrick. No. Why me, as in, why did you pick me to show yourself to? If what Harper says is true?"

Cute, she wants to feel special.

"I needed to get my dick wet. And scaring you first got it hard enough."

"You mean, you can't get your dick up unless you're scaring unwilling victims?" she throws back at me. Fucking bitch.

"No, you stupid little girl. Oh! You should know, your cunt is as dry as my brother's ashes." Now I'm an asshole.

Fallon stands up, turns around and looks up at where I'm leaning back on the branch and shouts, "You motherfucker!" I cut her off before she can continue, making it perfectly clear. "I have never fucked Joanie."

"You are unbelievable. No wonder my dad left this place. You and your mother are vile. Decency is not in your vocabulary. Either of you! I just lost the only family I had left. I was forced to come here. Assaulted by you and informed I can never fucking leave. I hate you and your mother!"

I move from the branch where I am comfortably lounging to the ground, dropping right in front of her.

"No one forced you to come here. I would have preferred if you'd never shown up at all, but it turns out we don't always get what we want. You could have found your lowlife, pathetic excuse of a mother. But no, you called Joanie instead. Someone who never wanted you and that you'd never met. And now you're just like the rest of us. Damned here for eternity."

Not wanting to hear another word from her annoying mouth, I grab hold of her neck and push her against the tree. She flinches at my touch, and I can only assume it's because her neck is still tender from the last time I held her like this.

Fallon's eyes go wide, and a worried look spreads across her face. I look her in the eye and raise my thumb to brush along her jawline. Her body unconsciously reacts, her chests heaves, eyes dilate, and she faintly bites her lip.

She likes this.

"So, are you just going to stand there, or are you going to do something about it?" Her eyes look down at my hard cock, then back up at me. Stupid little girl.

Brushing my face against the warmth of her skin, I bring my lips up to her ear. "I'll do whatever I fucking want. You'll regret coming here, and I will consume your regret. You can never escape. You did this to yourself. This is your life now, you stupid little girl."

Her breath hitches as she whispers back, "I hate you."

"Tell that to your body."

Moving my free hand, I bring it up to her waist and begin sliding it slowly down her leggings. Her back arches at my cool touch.

Fallon doesn't speak as I continue my slow descent to her bare pussy. My fingers brush along her lips. She is soaked.

"Fucking knew it. You are a little slut. A stupid little needy slut."

"Shut up," she hisses back.

Removing my hand from her pants, I grab her jaw. My fingers squeeze her face and I force her to look up at me. "You watch that fucking mouth of yours, or I will, while I'm skull fucking your face. Do you understand me, slut?"

With a slight nod from Fallon, I let go of her face, then her throat. Spinning her around so she faces the tree. "Don't you fucking move," I instruct her.

Undoing my pants, I pull them down to my knees and then kick her legs apart and pull her leggings down. There is no need for me to look at her face when all I require is her wet cunt.

Grabbing her hips, I pull them back towards me so she is bent at the waist. Lining my cock up with her entrance, I waste no time and slam into her.

She is drenched and my dick slides in without issue. I begin pounding into her tight pussy and hear a stifled moan leave her mouth.

"You will not cum. You do not deserve to cum. I saw you roll your eyes at me earlier. Such a bad little slut."

Determined to come first and leave her needy little cunt throbbing and yearning for release, I slam into her harder and faster. Fuck, she is so tight. My balls tighten as the familiar sensation begins to move down my spine.

"You will take all of it. Do you understand? Every fucking drop will stay inside your used pussy," grunting as my orgasm hits me. Fallon breathlessly answers, "Yes. Please, Merrick, fill my used pussy. Cum inside of me."

Ropes of my cum fill her, coating her cunt as I continue to work myself through my release. Chasing my orgasm, I don't let up. I can faintly hear the sound of my pelvis slapping against her skin, my hands still holding her waist to maintain control. Throwing my head back, "Fucking take it. Take it, you stupid little girl. You should have never come here. When you walk back to the house later, all you will feel is my cum dripping out of your pathetic pussy and regret filling your brain."

Thrusting into her one last time, my orgasm subsides. If my heart functioned, it would be racing and I would be out of breath. Perks of being a ghost, I suppose.

I pull out of her, letting go of her waist and see my cum already running down her leg. Fucking perfect.

Knowing she hasn't cum brings a satisfied smile to my face.

I pull my pants up and tuck myself back in, and she begins to do the same.

Neither of us speaks, until Fallon turns her head over her shoulder. "This is never happening again."

"It will if I say it will." I assure her before disappearing.

Stupid little girl, I will always make the rules.

CHAPTER 14
FALLON

Merrick hasn't shown up to torture or make me regret coming here in a few days. I ended up finishing myself off in the shower the other night after he denied my orgasm. Joke's on him. Aside from the glares I get from Joanie each time we pass or barely interact, it's been nice. I never thought I would say that about Port Canyon.

I've taken Harper's advice, and each chance I get, I am out in the graveyard. Instead of fighting my fate, I've decided to accept it. There is no escape. While it looks very appealing to sit here and be miserable about, instead I am going to try to befriend some ghosts.

Joanie is usually done for the day in the mid-afternoon, so she doesn't suspect anything. I wait and go in the evenings. The last thing I need is her finding out and adding more rat poison to my meals.

The sun has set, and the bright moon is helping to illuminate the graveyard along with some garden lights that are placed along the path. The past couple of nights, no one has come out, but I will not lose hope. I'm new to them. I'm sure they're as nervous as I am.

Wandering around the mausoleum, I run my hand along the rough surface of chipped stone and moss. It's beautiful in the night light.

I am about to move my hand off of it and my fingers catch on a ridge. As cold as the stone is, this is even cooler. I use both hands to clear the spongy, damp moss away. A dull bronze plaque appears under it with *Knight* engraved into it.

This is the family mausoleum.

Shocked, I step back.

My hands go to my chest. Eyes are wide.

I've gone from having no family to having them all here right in front of me. The feeling is over-whelming. One of the first thoughts I have is that I need to bring dad here. He needs to be with his family. Not held up in the house that he desperately escaped.

"Darling, you know what they say. If a boy picks on you, it means he likes you."

The older female voice catches me by surprise.

Turning to the direction it came from, I don't see anyone. "Hello?"

Coming out from behind a gravestone, an older lady with short black hair, a delicate and kind looking face and wearing a vintage-looking white lace dress, walks towards me.

"Merrick. That boy… He likes you, darling. That boy hasn't batted an eye at anyone in all his days here. Until you." She tells me.

I laugh at the outrageous statement, "Thank you for thinking so, but I assure you, he gets off on the torture." The lady shakes her head at me. "Ah, denial doesn't look good on you. But you seem to know that. We appreciate you wanting to spend time with us. You are the next keeper, so it's important we trust each other. We can tell you're genuine. We feel it. Your aura is pure. Unlike your grandmother. She is unkind to us and expects us to worship her. She believes without her, we would be doomed. But really, without us, she would be doomed. Her purpose would not exist. We coexist, like you both do in the main house."

I'm taken aback. How does she know that?

"We do not violate your privacy, Ms. Fallon. But we have seen your interactions and they are not kind ones. She resents you. For her and coming here. She knows you will take her place. She will murmur unkind things while here. The legacy is a privilege. She believes it is her right. It has consumed her and has turned her into a hateful woman."

The lady moves closer to me, but I'm not scared. I let her as she continues to speak.

"I am Darla Knight, your great grandmother three times over. I know what you're thinking, wow she has aged well," she says with a giggle. I like her.

"Joanie will not willingly pass the torch to you. She will not teach all there is to know. We see that. It's why we have come up with a plan. She is doing our family a disservice. Tarnishing all we worked for as a founding family. The next full moon is in a week. Just before the town opens itself up to the curious eyes. We must hold the ceremony then."

I look at her confused, "What do you mean? If she won't pass it down to me, how are we to hold the ceremony?"

Darla looks down at her feet, then back up at me. "We will help you. We will get her into the mausoleum where our family lies. You must do the hardest part, my girl. It will only work if you kill her during it, instead of only taking enough to fill the goblet."

"Absolutely not. I do not kill people! Are you insane?" I rapidly fire back.

"No, I am very serious. She will only become a bigger issue if she continues to live. In all our years, the bloodline legacy has never been broken. This is the only option.. We do not know what the town will do if we disobey tradition. Joanie has to go, and you have to take the helm. You can do this, Fallon. We see your determination. Instead of running scared, you have embraced us." She finishes explaining while gently taking my hand in hers in an attempt to comfort me.

"I understand, Darla–" but she cuts me off.

"Grandma, you may call me grandma." My chest feels warm, tears prick my eyes. I've never had a grandma before. Joanie made it very clear that she is not mine.

Damn you, Darla. You are good. Pulling at my heartstrings. It makes it nearly impossible to deny her.

Faintly, I whisper into the night, "I don't know if I can."

"Hush now. You can. We know you can. We believe in you, darling. We need you." Grandma Darla reassures.

Blowing out a deep breath, I close my eyes in disbelief that this is my life. In order to not break the legacy, the legend, and piss the town off, I have to murder my dad's mother during the next new moon. This is insane.

Opening my eyes, I look back at Darla, "Ok, what do I have to do?"

She smiles back at me, pleased with my response. "Tradition says, on the night of the full moon, you must enter the family mausoleum, wearing all black with the sacred ceremonial goblet. It is in that house, and you must find it. We will handle the rest. Don't you worry, we will be by your side the entire time."

This is fucking insane.

I have to do it. This is the only way. There is no way Joanie is going to do the right thing. Crusty, cold, miserable bitch that she is.

"In the meantime, you must spend more time in that library. You'll find all the details to prepare for new arrivals and everything else you need to know about being the keeper there." I nod my head in understanding.

"I'm going to go now, darling, but we will see each other again. I will be by your side when the time comes." With that, she is gone, disappearing into the night. My mind is racing a million miles a minute.

What have I agreed to? My thoughts are interrupted by a familiar voice.

"My feelings towards you are indifferent. I neither like you nor dislike you. I tolerate you. I agree with Darla, though. It has to happen on the next full moon before the town opens." I look up to find Merrick leaning against a tree with his black, worn combat boot-clad feet crossed at the ankles. With a lit joint between his fingers. Is he never not high?

"I cannot wait to see Joanie's face when she realizes what is happening. It will be worth a thousand deaths over. But you need to start researching, and learning your responsibilities, stupid little girl."

This fucker.

"I am trying. I will be ready! And stop calling me stupid little girl." I shout back at him.

Merrick laughs. "Try harder. I'll stop calling you stupid when you stop acting like it. Be smarter. Do better."

He is fucking unbelievable. "You don't want me here, but you want me to try harder. You want me to regret coming here, but insist I must do better. You fuck me, but insist I am pathetic. Can you please make up your fucking mind? My dad, your fucking brother, would be rolling over in his grave if he could see how you're treating me." Merrick is unfazed by my outburst. Instead, he takes another hit off his joint.

"It's a good thing he isn't in a grave then, since you burnt him. I have nothing to worry about." He takes another hit and continues, "You know what you have to do, so do it. The elders have spoken. It doesn't matter anymore what I want." He simply says before disappearing like Darla did.

I'm beginning to feel overwhelmed, but I can't let this feeling win. He's right. Though I will never admit that to him. A flash of bright light ignites in the distance, and Darla's voice comes back in my ear, "There is a storm coming, child. Best you get home."

The resounding crack of thunder vibrates through me.

Looking around the graveyard, I know she is right. It's for the good of the town. This has to be done. It is rather strange how calm I am about all of it. Maybe Harper is right, this is fate. Our destinies have always been written for us, and this is mine.

CHAPTER 15

FALLON

The rain began to fall heavily on my way back to the house. Pulling my hood over my head to not get completely soaked, I open the iron gate and continue my pursuit of warmth and a dry place. Making my way past the Angel of Death, another flash of lightning illuminates the sky. Glancing up at the house, I can see Joanie standing in the large window where the massive staircase is, watching me run through the deluge. Arms crossed and a scowl on her face.

Fuck.

Walking up the porch stairs and into the house, I am soaked.

There is no way I can cower off and hide. I have to walk up those stairs and face Joanie.

My shoes squeak on the tile. Approaching the stairs, she belts out, "What did I tell you?"

Here we go.

"I was out for a walk when it started raining," I say, playing stupid. It's my last ditch effort to avoid a confrontation with this nasty woman, and hopefully direct her suspicions elsewhere.

"I told you to mind your business and not to go snooping. Why were you beyond the hedges?" Looking down at my feet, I keep to my story. "I was just out for a walk, Joanie. I wasn't snooping."

"LIAR!"

I look back up at her and my already racing heart goes a little faster.

Fuck me. This is not the time.

Merrick is standing behind her. His index finger pressed against his lips, gesturing for me to not give away his presence.

Keeping my face neutral, "I'm not lying." It's a pathetic response, but I don't want to sound defensive. She would definitely call my bluff if I did.

Another flash of lightning brightens the room. Merrick has moved his hand, his thumb is moving across his throat in a slicing motion. His tongue is out and as he reaches the end, he flops his head to the side.

"I am watching you, girl," she says dismissively before turning her back to me and going up the stairs to her wing of the house.

She is so fucking on to me. I'll need to be more careful now. She cannot find out what's going to happen until it does or we are all fucked.

MERRICK

Fallon wastes no time rushing up the staircase once Joanie leaves. She doesn't even acknowledge me as she passes.

Like that will stop me.

I beat her to her room, making myself comfortable on her large bed, waiting for her to arrive. I hear the floorboards creak as she gets closer. The bedroom door swings open, she spots me instantly. "Get the fuck out of my room."

"Are you on your period?"

She slams the door closed behind her. "I cannot fucking stand you. You are arrogant. You totally disregard others people's feelings every time you open your fucking mouth. I wish you never showed yourself to me. Just leave me alone!"

"Stupid little girl sees an elder spirit, gets a little power, and thinks she can speak to me like that?" I say, then transport myself, so I'm standing right in front of her. The bruise that was once prominent around her neck is almost completely faded. That's too bad. I liked it there.

Before she even sees me move, my hand is wrapped around her throat. Cutting off her air supply. She balls up her fists and punches my arm to get me to let go. Not fucking happening. I squeeze even tighter, and she begins wheezing. Her punches have less of an impact and tears run down her soft cheeks.

I force her to the ground, and she bends her knees, unable to fight back. Her eyes pleading with me to stop, but that only fuels me even more.

I release my grip on her throat and she begins coughing, taking in huge gulps of air, trying to fill her lungs. She places her hands on the floor in front of her for balance, and it's then I notice her clothes are still soaked from the rain, not that I care.

Undoing my pants, I pull out my cock, already hard from squeezing her throat and watching her pathetic eyes pleading with me to stop. "Stay on your knees, slut. You're fucking desperate for my cock aren't you? You're fighting it so hard that it's painfully obvious."

Fallon looks up at me, her face still red from the

lack of oxygen. "Get it away from me," she pathetically whispers. It only makes me want it more.

"Now where would the fun in that be, stupid little girl?" I question back. I love that she is fighting back. It makes it that much more fun for me.

"The more you struggle, the harder I get. Now, open that desperate mouth of yours," I demand.

She resists, but still, I bring the tip of my cock to her lips. It's already leaking precum as I rub it along her mouth. Leaving her lips glistening.

Forcing it between her pouty lips, they reluctantly open, wrapping around my head. Fuck, this feels amazing. I haven't had a blowjob since before I died.

Grabbing the back of her head, I thrust myself further into her mouth and down her throat. Through hooded eyes, I watch her take all of me in. With each movement, I get deeper, making her gag. I pinch her nostrils together, and she struggles even more. Her body convulsing, begging for air. It's fucking beautiful.

"You're hungry for it, aren't you, slut?" I growl at her, continuing my assault of her mouth. She hollows her cheeks, sucking me harder as drool runs out of her mouth. Fuck. I throw my head back. This is fucking incredible.

My stomach muscles contract as my body tingles.

Spurred on, I thrust faster into her warm mouth. Chasing my building orgasm.

Then ropes of my warm cum shoot out and down her throat. "Fucking take it, slut. Take all of it." I rasp at her as I continue to fill her mouth with my seed.

My movements slow and still holding her head, I push myself as far as I can down her throat and hold it there. Making sure she gets everything. Not wasting a drop. She will fucking take it all. She's gagging even more and I can feel her trying to gasp for air. Holding myself like this a moment longer, my orgasm dies, and I begin to pull out and let go of her head.

As I pull my cock out of her mouth, her swollen lips slide down my shaft. Fallon sucks in a breath of air through her nose, then swallows her build up of saliva and my cum.

Her body is shaking as she sits up on her knees and moves backwards until her back hits her bedroom door. I put my cock back in my pants, doing them up, and look at her beautifully frightened face.

"You are pure evil," she hisses.

"I gifted you my giant cock and cum. I think you're misdirecting your anger. Joanie is the one you're pissed at. Not me." Fuck, I do not have the energy for this.

Fallon rolls her eyes at me, before closing them and taking in calculated breaths.

That's a good girl. No need to continue this battle, you'll lose anyway.

"You've never asked how my dad died."

Her statement catches me off guard.

"That's what you're thinking about after sucking my cock?" *What the fuck?* "It's irrelevant how he died. He is dead. It's done."

She sits in silence, surely not shocked by my callous response. She has to know me well enough by now to know I'm not going to sugarcoat shit for her.

I rake my fingers through my white hair. "Port Canyon doesn't cremate their dead. The bodies go into the earth intact to assist them in their transition. There's never been ashes of the dead before, that I know of. It makes me wonder… What kind of form or shape he will be in when his spirit decides to show up? Ya know?" I pause for a moment when an idea comes to mind. "Maybe Mark will be like Voldermort when he turns to sand at the ministry?"

Fallon growls her frustration. She is about to fucking blow. And I am so here for it.

Walking over to my brother's ashes, examining his urn, this is what he's been reduced to. I'm proud he got out, but disappointed. It was all for nothing.

Looking back at Fallon, she goes to speak, but stops herself a couple of times. She's biting her tongue.

She desperately wants to engage and challenge me, but is fighting it so hard. She knows I get off on it. Too bad I know she does, too.

"Ok. So, you mean he could still come back and be like you?"

Didn't I just suggest that?

"Wow, you really don't miss a thing. Do you? Of course he will, eventually. You read the book. You've heard the stories. Come on, catch up, stupid little girl."

Fallon stands up from the ground on shaky legs, she is shivering more now. Still in her rain-soaked clothing that I haven't given her the chance to change out of.

Her finger pokes at my chest. "Stop. Calling. Me. Stupid. Little. Girl!" she shouts at me.

"Then stop being one. It's that easy, Fallon. Be smarter. Do better." I snap back.

Fuck, I do not want to engage in a pointless argument with her. She is tired and frustrated and overwhelmed by all the information that's been thrown at her lately.

"Here's some advice, a hint, if you will, but only because we don't have much time." I tell her.

"There is no we, *uncle*," she throws back at me.

Looking down into her dark eyes. "The goblet… it's in Joanie's room. There's no we, so I wish you the best of luck.. You won't need my help."

Not waiting to see her reaction, I leave and go back to my room. Settling on my bed, lighting a joint and taking a hit, I stare up at the ceiling, cross my feet at my ankles, and place a hand behind my head. The satisfied grin that spreads across my face is knowing, malicious, *expectant*.

I can't wait to see her crawling toward me. Begging for my help, '*Oh, please Merrick. Please help me.*'

Because that's the only way I'll agree to it.

CHAPTER 16

MERRICK

J oanie is out. I saw her leave earlier, off to the town center. She likes to walk the ten minutes once a week to do whatever it is she does there. I don't fucking care.

Fallon has Harper over and they are in the attic, catching her up on the events of the last twenty-four hours while going through trunks of all the shit.

"What if I don't want this, Harper? What if I just want to leave, and never look back? I didn't sign up for this. I'm scared and I feel trapped," Fallon complains to Harper. Here we go. Welcome to the pity party.

How many times does this girl need to be told she can't fucking leave. The town let my brother think he got away. Fuck, I thought *I* got away.

Guess who's back?

Me. My brother and now you, stupid little girl. The town got a deal, three for the price of two.

"Fallon. It's not that bad. I love it here. Maybe one day you will love it too, with time." Harper suggests.

Fallon sits with it, but she's not as subtle as she thinks. "Tell me. The last new person to come and live here was what, over fifty years ago? Why did the town let them in? If I ask nicely, will it let me leave?"

Fuck this. I can't handle this bullshit anymore.

"Fallon, you are next in line. Plans are already in motion. There is no leaving. As much as I'd love to be the reason you'd try, it won't happen. A part of you believes the curse. If you didn't, you would have already tried."

Harper's eyes are wide, and her jaw goes slack.

"Fuck you, Merrick. Fuck this. Harper, let's go."

"...but. No. Merrick?" Harper stutters.

"Obviously."

I don't have time for two stupid little girls.

"The last person to move here had something to offer the town. The elders at the time voted on it and they allowed her to stay. That shit is rare."

"He's right. She pleaded her case at the bridge and they let her enter. She brought with her the love for

Port Canyon, which was solely based on the rumors and whispers. It didn't scare her. She said she would do anything to be a part of us. The elders decided she could stay, but they would arrange a marriage for her in order to produce heirs for the aging Healer. He has been so consumed with his practice that he hadn't taken the time to find someone. The marriage was arranged and multiple heirs were produced. Everyone here serves a purpose. No one stays here by accident."

Interrupting Harper, I add my two cents. "She basically signed on to be a glorified whore. A baby producer extraordinaire."

"Is he always like this?" Harper questions, and Fallon is quick to snark back. "Yes. This is actually tame, considering."

"Aw, a compliment. I knew I was growing on you, but I don't fall for stupid little girls." I tease back, knowing this will only further piss her off.

"You know what? I think you should try running. Let me chase you to the bridge. See what happens. Will the town curse you right away or edge you like they did with my brother? Drawing it out until the very end, then bam! Dead. Gone forever. And they still got him back. They got you too." I throw at her, smiling.

Fallon stands and rushes me, getting right in my

face, and I swear I see a glimmer of sadness in her dark eyes. "You don't know shit. You left my dad here alone. With your mother. You are a fucking coward. My dad tried. He fucking tried! You gave up, driving yourself off a bridge. You see that car down there?" Fallon points to the tower window that looks down to the driveway. "My dad, your fucking baby brother, searched for ages to find that car. A 1985 Porsche. To honor your memory. To feel fucking closer to you. You are pathetic." Fuck me. She played the sentimental card, well played. Keeping my face neutral, not wanting her to see she's affected me, "Do you feel better? Getting all that out?" I question her. As much as I want to watch her run from me, to push her further, to take pride in breaking her into a million tiny pieces, we don't have fucking time. The spirit elders have given her a timeline.

Moving quickly, I pin her to the wall. Dust rises upon impact, misting over us.

"Stop being so fucking dramatic and focus! We don't have time for this shit, Fallon!"

"Gonna choke me again?" she says defiantly. Taunting me while arching her pelvis up to mine. My cock is hard beneath my pants.

"You're desperate for it, aren't you? Craving my cum dripping out of your pussy while I have you pinned here. Harper watching. You are fucking filthy."

Clearing her throat, Harper begins tapping her foot on the dusty wood floor. "As cute as this angry foreplay is, I did not pay for this subscription, Merrick. Let her go because I think I found the perfect initiation outfit. Fallon, get over here."

Before I let Fallon go, I place my free hand on her pant-clad pussy, "You. Are. Soaking. Fucking. Wet. I knew it, desperate slut," I whisper in her ear before stepping back and letting her go and disappearing.

The need to destroy her, make her bend and scream has only heightened, withered and trembled from my touch and fear. I can't explain it other than I'm fucked in the head. But what she said earlier ignited a fire inside of me and not the way she hoped for.

Fucking bitch. I didn't leave my brother. I showed him how important it was to get out. Obviously, I didn't know then what I do now. But what's done is done.

Blood for blood.

FALLON

Nothing good happens when Merrick pops up,

and this time was no different. He thrived on having Harper here. It gave him an audience for his bullshit.

I let him see he was getting to me.

I'm so fucking weak. That bastard. Bringing up my dad.

"Fallon, focus. Look," Harper shouts impatiently at me. Turning around, I snap, "What!"

Her face drops as she continues holding up the black corset bodysuit she wanted to show me.

"I'm sorry. Merrick... He knows how to push my buttons, and I'm sorry. Show me. What did you find? Please." Harper nods, "I know. I can feel your tension from here. It's ok, Fal. Let's forget him and focus on this!" She bounces on the balls of her feet with renewed excitement.

Harper holds out the black fabric to me and I gently take it, unsure of how old it could be. Joanie definitely would not be caught rocking this.

The black corset bodysuit with thin shoulder straps, lined with black rhinestones, is absolutely stunning. I rub my fingers over it in amazement. Turning it over, I notice it's a thong. What naughty ancestor was wearing this? The thought makes me smile. The backing has rows of loose, thick black ribbon waiting to be tightened.

"Fal, this could be perfect and it looks your size.

Let me take this home. I have the perfect thing to go with it." Harper is beaming. How can I turn down that face?

"Ok, let's do this. But wait, you can sew?" Questioning back with a raised eyebrow. This is so delicate, I would hate for it to be ruined.

"I sew up dead people for a living. How much harder could this be, really?" Oh sweet Jesus, my eyes widen. Sewing clothes is a little different from sewing dead people, but I can't ruin her excitement and decide to go with it, "Alright. That settles it."

Harper rushes me, wrapping her arms around me squealing, "You won't regret this! Thank you."

Right. The outfit has been found and being handled.

Now for the impossible task of getting that fucking goblet away from Joanie.

CHAPTER 17
MERRICK

"Fallon! You think you can come in here and make a goddamn mess of everything?" Joanie announces her arrival.

Harper left some time ago and Fallon has had her head buried in the books, reading up on the town's history and searching for family information.

How fucking boring.

"FALLON!" Joanie screams at the top of her lungs. Here come the fireworks. I'm sitting on the staircase that goes to Joanie's wing, leaning back on my elbows with my legs extended and crossed at the ankles. She can't see me. She will never fucking see me.

Fallon runs out of her room where she was reading and rushes down the grand staircase, stopping at the landing where they part in two directions, and stands there in her black sweatpants and oversized white tee. Her hair is in a high messy pony. The girl is gorgeous. I'll give her that much. Her button nose, pouty lips, and the smattering of freckles that bridge over her nose.

"You think this shit is funny, Fallon?" Joanie snarks. Fallon's brows furrow in confusion.

Shaking her head, "What are you talking about?"

Ladies and gentlemen, welcome to the main attraction.

You're probably thinking, *what have you done now, Merrick? Why can't you just be nice to Fallon? She's been through enough.* Boo fucking hoo. Where would the fun be in that?

Now, stop asking stupid fucking questions and see for yourself.

"Your goddamn car has made a mess of the driveway. What in the hell were you thinking?"

"I've been inside all day. I have no idea what you're talking about." Fallon defends herself.

"Don't play stupid with me. Your little act may have worked on your father, but it won't work with me." Oh, dead daddy has been brought up, touchy subject. This should go over well. I smile while biting my lip.

"You dumb bitch. Hear the words coming out of my mouth. I. Haven't. Done. Shit. To. Your. Fucking. Driveway. I've been upstairs with my headphones in." Fuck, yes. I sit up and rub my hands together in anticipation.

The big reveal is coming. Just call me the next Picasso or whatever his fucking name is.

"You are truly a filthy, vulgar girl. Waste at the bottom of the bin," Joanie insults Fallon further. Fallon doesn't stick around to hear anymore of it. She whips past me on the stairs towards Joanie's wing, and I follow in hot pursuit. Where in the fuck is she going? It doesn't matter, we cannot miss a moment people, keep the cameras rolling!

I worked too fucking hard this afternoon, making it just right.

The click of the locks unlatching tells me she is heading to the second floor terrace that overlooks the front driveway. A bird's eye fucking view. Even better.

The door slams open, bouncing off the side of the house as Fallon storms to the balcony ledge. She turns slowly, her face is beat red with nostrils flaring, "You bastard. You piece of shit. I know you're here. You fucking coward, show yourself!" Fallon glares around, casting her eyes to find me.

Joanie walks out with a smirk on her face.

"Daddy won't save you now, sweetheart. You are done. You think I haven't noticed your sudden interest in the cemetery? The library and the missing books? This will seal your coffin, destroying the place. Their home. They will never want you. You are nothing more than a disrespectful, spoiled little bitch! Even your father died to get away from you."

Yes, Joanie, and I drove off a fucking bridge to get away from you. What's the old saying about stones and glasshouses, Joanie?

This, what Joanie just said, pushes Fallon over the edge. Her face goes even redder, her chest is heaving, and she's clenching her fists. She's going to punch Joanie. Fuck, this is going better than I could have ever imagined.

Before Fallon can act on her anger, Joanie shocks the shit out of both of us. Walking up to Fallon, she tightly grabs onto her ponytail and pulls it down so Fallon's head follows. Joanie looks down at her and whispers, "You ungrateful bitch," then slaps her across the face. The crack of her palm connecting with Fallon's cheek reverberates in the small space. A murderous shriek comes from Fallon's mouth when Joanie tightens her grip on Fallon's hair.

I did not think this would escalate the way it did.

Screw it.

Walking up to Joanie, I wrap my hand around her throat, forcing her backward, and she lets go of Fallon. I squeeze tighter and she reaches up to her neck in a desperate attempt to remove my hand, but it won't work. Pushing her back until we reach the edge where the black iron bars wrap around the balcony, I lift her off the ground and her legs kick out in the air, tears streaming down her face.

Fallon rushes toward me; she knows I could very well kill Joanie right now. When she gets to me, I push her back with my other arm. The force shoots her backwards where she falls into the floor to ceiling windows lining the area, and her head bounces off the glass paneling. Fallon holds the back of her head with a scowl on her face. Her eyes look sad, like she's hurt. I don't have time to focus on her right now. If I had blood, it would be boiling.

I glance once more at Fallon, checking that she's alright.

Focusing back on Joanie, I finally show myself. If my hand wasn't cutting off her air, she'd gasp in shock. I have her hanging over the balcony with nothing but stone to catch her twenty feet below. The only thing stopping her from falling to her death is me.

Now, before you say it... I know. I'm so strong and manly, holding her life in my fucking hands. About time. In my opinion, being a ghost has its perks.

Too bad now is not her time. That honor is reserved for Fallon, who more than fucking deserves the privilege.

"Touch her again, and I'll drop you. Talk to her again, and I'll drop you. Don't go fucking near her. Understood?" Joanie is losing strength. I can feel her growing weaker with each slap against my arm.

"Nod your fucking head. Do you understand? Don't make this so easy. Because I will fucking drop you." I shout at her, and she nods twice with wide eyes.

Hoisting her back over the railing, I drop her to the floor in front of me, and it takes all my willpower not to make her lick my boots as well. To make her feel worthless. My cock hardens at the thought of it.

Hold up. Rewind.

My cock does not get hard for Joanie. Let's get that fucking clear right now.

The bitch is so evil that once Fallon ends her, even the Devil won't want her.

Now, back to my dick. It gets hard from the

thought of making her feel tiny, worthless, and like the waste of space she is. That shit gets me off.

Not Joanie. Never is it Joanie.

"You asshole. That hurt." Fallon shouts from behind me. I take my gaze off Joanie and turn around to see Fallon. She is rubbing the back of her head where her ponytail once was.

Is this chick serious?

When I am being an asshole, she'll know it. And that was not one of those moments.

Now folks, let's get to the reason we are all up here. Yeah, it's a complete asshole move, but also fucking hilarious.

I turn my focus back on Joanie.

"This is the first and last time you will ever see me. I didn't show myself for you. So, you can stop building yourself up like I did. It was for her," pointing back to Fallon. "Now get up and fuck off."

Joanie's is speechless, which is fucking rare.

"Are you deaf? Get the fuck up and go!"

She stumbles getting up, tears still running down her face. She coughs a couple of times and then scurries toward the open door.

"Oh, and by the way, that shit in the driveway was me. Not Fallon. So, fuck you and your fucking driveway." I shout at her and hold both my middle fingers up at her.

She turns her head to look at me and mutters under her breath, "You were always my least favorite."

I can't wait for Fallon to kill the bitch, honestly. Fuck, this town—this world—will all be a better place for it.

Taking my hands, I rub them both down my face, feeling exasperated by her presence. "Joanie. Do you ever shut up?" She disappears inside after that.

I'm about to leave after a job well done, when Fallon's voice catches my attention.

"You prick. How did you get my keys?" she asks from where she is standing, looking over the ledge.

Ah yes! My masterpiece. It's one of a kind. I don't make the same shit twice.

"Do you like it? Not bad, right?"

"What is it supposed to be?" she questions.

"A fucking dick. The balls are the two donuts and the long curved part is the dick. Are your eyes even open? How do you not see that?" Pointing at each element while explaining. I know this girl isn't thick in the head, but fuck me, the cock and balls are perfectly traced tire marks on the cobblestone driveway.

Fallon turns to face me. "Don't touch my car again. That's all I have left of my dad. If anything were to happen to it... Just stop touching my stuff! You make me so fucking mad, Merrick."

"Your keys are already back where I found them." I say before disappearing.

Alright kids. The show is over.

It was fun while it lasted. Tune in next time where I will teabag Fallon in her sleep for being so fucking cute when she's mad.

CHAPTER 18

FALLON

Fucking inconsiderate asshole.

Touching my car. His brother's car. After all the low blows and jabs he's made. Disgusting.

This is who he is. Who he will always be.

Finally, I'm back in my room and the floor is still covered in books and random papers I found in the attic. Harper and I pored over them so I can learn as much as I need to before the ceremony.

As much as I didn't ask for this responsibility, it is mine. Based on what I have found in the books, everything they have told me about not being able to leave seems to be true.

A part of me wants to see if something happens if I try, but I also don't want to be cursed for trying.

"Fallon! What is going on over here?" Harper shouts down the hallway, and I hear the pounding of her footsteps against the floor.

Harper looks panicked when she rushes through my door. "I heard yelling and screaming. Then I saw a deformed penis on the driveway. Joanie must be pissed!"

Walking over to Harper, I wrap my arms around her. She hesitates for a second, but hugs me back. I'm exhausted. I've been holding myself up alone for the past few weeks since dad died and I'm just so damn tired. I need someone to hold me for a bit.

My head hurts. My cheek is throbbing, and my back aches from being pushed into the window.

Releasing her, I walk over to my bed and sit crossed leg, and Harper joins me.

"Merrick." Is all I need to say. She gets it.

"So that was his art he added to the driveway then?" I only nod in response. "How pissed was Joanie?"

Shaking my head, I blow out a deep breath. "She was livid. She came home and was screaming *'Fallon'* and I didn't hear her because my headphones were in while I was reading all the stuff we found upstairs about my family and the town. Then she kept shouting and when I finally heard her, I came running down and you would have thought I had thrown pig's blood all over the place with how pissed she was. Then, we went to the second-floor balcony, because I obviously had no idea what she was going on about. She kept blabbing on saying the most vile things about me and my dad. I wanted to punch her. I wanted to punch her so badly, but before I could, she pulled on my hair and slapped me! I couldn't comprehend what happened, and the next thing I know, Merrick was holding her over the ledge." Harper's jaw drops as I continue. "I rushed them, because I thought he was definitely going to drop her, but he forced me back into the house. I ended up slamming against the windowsill and hitting my head. Now I have one hell of a headache. He brought her back over, told her off some more and when she goes to leave, he tells her the driveway was him and she snarks on about him always being her least favorite. Joanie is pure evil. I mean, Merrick is an absolute ass, but there is no need to say that to your child. It's no wonder him and my dad risked it all and tried to get out any way they could." I shake my head at the thought. The woman is a witch. A witch I get to kill.

At first, the thought repulsed me. I'm not a killer. I have had angry thoughts before, but never felt the urge to act upon them. After today though, I'm excited to end her life. I'll take her spot and watch the light leave her eyes as I drink from the goblet.

The goblet. Shit. We still need to get that.

Harper can tell I'm lost in my own thoughts when she interrupts, "Earth to Fallon. Finish the story please," she pleads.

"Right. Sorry. So once I saw what he did, I was livid. He touched my car. He stole my keys, drove my car and did that shit. He makes me so angry all the time. What was really interesting was when he got all high and mighty with Joanie and told her she is not to speak to me or look at me. Since when did he care if people were nice to me or not? The guy gets off on torturing me. It doesn't make sense."

"It makes perfect sense. He likes you!" Harper is way too giddy right now. Bouncing her bum on the bed with the biggest smile.

"No. Not a chance. Darla said the same thing. He legitimately gets off on being a dick. No feelings are involved other than that when talking about him." I laugh at her. "Can we not talk about him anymore, please? I'm honestly so exhausted. Everything is catching up with me, and it's overwhelming. I've been studying and getting ready for the ceremony, but what if I'm not good enough?"

Harper's hand touches my leg. "Stop that

thinking right now. You're tired. Your brain is tricking you into thinking things that aren't true. Nothing a good night's sleep can't fix. But first, your dress, I'm almost done! It is simply exquisite, if I say so myself. You are going to look hot. You can thank me later. I should be done in another two or three days, tops!" This girl was right. She is my best friend.

"Thank you, Harper. Not just for the dress, but for everything."

"Don't be silly. I told you we would be best friends!" What a sassy bitch. Gloating. She is gloating. Taking a pillow, I toss one at her face and we both break into laughter. It feels good. I needed this.

I bet she knew that, too.

"Wait…The ceremony. Shouldn't we tell the other town elders? Don't they need to be there for it? I haven't even met them. It will be nearly impossible to sneak around that much without Joanie flipping her shit again."

"Chill. Darla and I got this handled."

"What do you mean, you and Darla?"

"Darla and I go way back. She's my girl, too. Don't get jealous, you're still my number one. When I was hanging out there the other day, she asked dad and I to let them know as discreetly as possible.

Which we have been doing. They will be here the next full moon."

"Thank you! I'm nervous to meet them. Is that normal?"

"Of course it is. But they are just like you and I. It will be fine. Everything will work out. Darla has been planning along with the other spirits on how to get Joanie into the mausoleum. The elders are on the same page. Soon you will have the dress and the goblet and we will be all set! You can do this, Fallon. I believe in you, and I need you to believe in you!"

Nodding my head, "I'm having an off day. You're right, I need to sleep. As long as you're there too, I'll be fine. I just need a familiar face with me. Will you stand next to me?"

"Of course I will! You're not doing this alone. One day I will take over for my dad and I will need you next to me too." Harper reaches in for another hug. I didn't think I was a hugger, but she is really good at it.

When she pulls back, I almost don't want to let her. "Ok, I'm going to go. You rest! Tomorrow maybe spend the day in the graveyard when Joanie isn't there. It's kind of relaxing, and you can get to know more spirits. I love you!"

"I love you too." I smile back at her. She gets up

from the bed and walks to the door. Flicking off my light, she demands, "Sleep!" Then shuts my door.

I really do love that girl. I'm not sure I would have survived this far if it wasn't for her.

Morning sun creeps through my curtains.

Rubbing my eyes, I grab my phone to check the time. It's already 10:30am, having slept ten hours, I feel refreshed. I roll over to turn on the lamp and... What the fuck?

I need to touch it to make sure it's real and I'm not dreaming.

My finger brushes alongside it, and the silver is cold against my skin. Shiny red rubies line the center and appear to go all the way around. Intricate designs run along the stem.

It's real.

It's the fucking goblet from Joanie's room. How did it end up here, in my room?

CHAPTER 19
MERRICK

And you all thought chivalry was dead.

Yeah, I got the goblet for her.

Not because I felt bad for what happened earlier in the day. I thoroughly enjoyed that. Possibly a little too much. I ended up having to have one off the wrist afterward. Holding Joanie's pathetic body in the air like that. What a fucking dream it was.

Moving on from that.

The goblet. The infamous goblet.

Did I want her to try to get into Joanie's room and fail?

Yes.

Did I want her to plead for my help? Get on her knees and beg, '*Oh, please, Merrick, please will you help me? I'll suck your dick.*' That last bit is greedy hope, considering each of our prior sexual encounters were initiated by me, and her not exactly enjoying it.

Of course, I want her to beg for my help, and there is still time for that. She doesn't even need to beg willingly. As long as she's on her knees, I'll take it.

Anyway….

Back to the goblet and why I am so nice.

Honestly, I couldn't take another minute of her fucking moaning and groaning.

Anything to shut the girl up. If that includes shoving my cock in her mouth, then so be it. I'll fucking do it. Next time, there will be no goblet to save her tonsils.

Once I heard my stupid little girl and Harper having their girl talk, I had to get the fuck out of there. So now I'm in the cemetery sitting on the grass, smoking a joint behind one of the taller tombstones. The base is a large, thick square with a statue of an angel holding its heart standing on top of it. If anyone were to come down here, they wouldn't be able to see me.

Can't smoke a joint in my ghost form, now can I?

My legs are bent at the knee. Both my wrists resting on top of them with the burning joint squeezed between thumb and forefinger. The hood of my black zip up hoodie is up and pieces of my white hair are falling over my eyes.

I can't help but think of the afternoon; it felt amazing being behind the wheel again. It took me back to that night on the bridge. For the first time since dying, I felt alive. Felt what must have been phantom adrenaline rushing through my body, and now I'm coming down from that high and replacing it with another.

Your good pal Merrick is about to be vulnerable for a minute, folks. This will be the first and last fucking time. I'm not a pussy and I'll deny this entire conversation.

When Joanie was telling Fallon off, it brought me so much joy. It was hilarious. Fallon was so fucking confused. It was funny as fuck.

Until it wasn't.

Something clicked inside me on that balcony.

Only I get to talk to her that way. Anyone else, I would murder. Which is what almost happened to Joanie. If she wasn't meant for my stupid little girl, then I would have dropped her.

Her screams filling the air.

Her head smashing into the stone driveway.

Blood running out of her mouth and broken bits of skull.

Her brain being eaten by crows.

I may have daydreamed about this a time or two.

Sue me.

At least I'm honest about it, unlike you fuckers.

But now, it's my brain that's messed up instead of Joanie's. And I hate it.

"Now, Merrick. Don't make me mother you." Ah, here comes the noisy and self-proclaimed mom of the cemetery, Darla.

"Now, why would I want to stop you from doing the only thing you seem to be decent at?" I can feel her shaking her head at me. But since when have I cared?

"You like the girl. My granddaughter. If you fight it any longer, you will lose her. If you push her too far, she won't come back."

Taking a hit, my head tilts up to the sky as I blow it out. "She shouldn't have come here. This fucking town just takes and takes. What does it ever give back? It's bullshit, just like your theory." Turning my head slightly to look in her direction, "And don't forget, I'm your grandkid too, old lady."

"I haven't forgotten. But sometimes you need a firm hand which needs to come from the un-grand-motherly side of me. Like right now. You may think she is a stupid little girl, but you are acting like a stupid little boy."

I left the main house to get away from moaning voices, only to turn up here to have Darla in my ear.

Fuck me.

"Merrick. It's time you pull your head out of your own ass and see what is right in front of you. You have never put this much effort into pissing someone off before; and you haven't ever done anything nice for anyone, unless there was an ulterior motive. That goblet was not that. You have appeared for her. Don't think I don't know about the other stuff, either. You like Fallon. It's about time you accept that." Does she ever shut up?

"Now put your stinky drugs away and do something about it before you go too far. Before you lose her for good. Which you are very close to doing, stupid little boy." This woman needs to find a hobby that isn't my life.

"Have you seen my dear old dad lately?" Changing the subject before she makes me give a shit about what she's rambling on about.

"No. He hasn't shown himself in years. Just like you, he's always running away or hiding." I walked right into this. I've successfully stayed hidden for thirty years until now. Dear old dad pops in once in a while, but he has never seen me. He watches from a distance, keeping to himself in the graveyard. And like me, he has never shown himself to Joanie.

She destroyed this family.

Now it's the family's turn to destroy her.

Putting my joint out under my boot, I get up from where I'm sitting. "Good chat, Darla. Let's never do this again, yeah?"

"I'll let you be mean to me, but only because I know what I've said affects you. You think about it, I know you do. Don't mistake my kindness for weakness, boy. I could kick your ass whenever I wanted."

"Sounds like a good time. And possibly like a come on... care to share your feelings with the class?" She's definitely going to kick my ass now.

"Get out of here, Merrick, and fix this. Don't fuck up your one chance of actual happiness." Darla disappears after that.

Frustrating old bat.

She's right though. Fuck, I hate it. Reaching my hands up to my hair, I grab a bunch of it and pull it. Hard.

It helps me focus. It keeps intrusive thoughts at bay and I don't want to deal with them yet.

Fuck.

It's not working. Goddammit.

I walk over to the family mausoleum and run my fingers against the cold iron door. I haven't been inside since I died.

I grab the handle and turn the knob, hearing the click of the latch. Pushing the heavy door open, I go inside. The space is cold and damp, and the air feels stale. Normally I would go through the walls of places, but this seems more significant. I'm feeling sentimental tonight.

It's dark. Cement tombs line the walls on either side of me. Reaching out, my hands brush against them.

My body is in the one to the left. It doesn't feel like thirty years.

Every memory feels like this all happened recently. Time has escaped me.

Taking in my surroundings, I start to picture what it will look like in here in a few days. Fallon will be in here taking her crown.

The mental image of Joanie's blood coating the floor is already satisfying. I can't wait for the main event.

A million other thoughts are riddling me.

There's only one thing left to do.

I've already driven myself off a bridge, so that's not an option.

CHAPTER 20
MERRICK

H er lips are slightly parted as her chest slowly rises with each breath.

Fallon is in her sleep shorts and tee with her right hand slightly under the waistband and her blankets bunched at her feet.

Tilting my head, it makes me wonder what she is thinking?

When I used to sleep, it only meant one thing.

Maybe she's dreaming of my giant cock impaling her tight cunt. Maybe not, but what other reason could she have to sleep like this?

Whatever.

Not that my curiosity matters, anyway.

Grabbing my switchblade from my pants pocket, I

flip it open and place the cool metal blade between my teeth, and my lips close against it.

Then, placing one knee on the edge of her bed, I let it get used to my weight so as not to alert her. Once I'm sure I haven't woken her, I bring my other knee up and rest it on the mattress.

Leaning forward, I place both hands down on either side of her body. I watch her breathing, and it still hasn't changed. Her chest continues to rise in the same steady rhythm.

Grabbing the blade out of my mouth, I bring it to her sleep shorts. The blade is sharp. I've kept it in pristine condition, what I am about to do will require minimal effort.

Moving slowly, I place the tip of the blade against the crotch of her shorts and move it up the seam. As I slice open her shorts, I focus on her face. Watching for any sudden movements or signs that she was waking up. My blade slices through the thin fabric like butter. The room fills with the scent of Fallon, my desperate little slut.

My eyes widen, and my movements stop.

What the fuck.

MY desperate little slut. Fuck me. Is Fallon mine?

No. I referred to her as MY stupid little girl at least once today in the cemetery, too.

Shit. No.

I'm judging myself right now, too. Don't worry team.

My face scrunches in disgust. Like I'm stuck in a room where someone just shit themselves.

Nope. Not today. Not right now. Back to focusing on what is in front of me.

The tightest pussy known to mankind. It's like one of those goddamn finger traps. I stick my cock in it and the more I try to pull out, the tighter it gets.

I finish moving the blade up to where her fingers rest on her pelvis. Slowly and quietly, I flip it closed and slide it back into my front pant pocket.

Running two fingers up the opening, I can feel her soft bare skin underneath. She isn't wearing any panties. Moving my fingers between her lips, she's wet. Someone is having naughty dreams. Maybe she is my desperate little slut after all.

My one finger finds her sensitive clit and I tease it, slowly circling it a few times. Her breath hitches, and her pelvis moves slightly to the rhythm of it. Not wanting to wake her, I stop, focusing back on her swollen lips. Rubbing my fingers gently between them, her wet cunt drips on them, lubricating them enough that I can push them inside of her with minimal resistance.

Stopping once I get one knuckle deep, her other hand moves to her chest while the one already under her waistband moves further down. Using my other hand, I undo my pants and free my hard cock.

Satisfied that she is still asleep, I push my fingers in more and gently rub her tight walls, looking for that tricky little monster, the G-Spot. My desperate little slut's hips move and I know I have found it.

Her cunt continues to drench my fingers with each time I rub against it. A shallow moan escapes from between her lips, and precum drips from my cock.

She is going to fucking kill me when she figures out what I have done. Good thing I've already handled that part myself.

I pull my fingers out, and her pussy releases them with ease. I bring them up to her face and gently brush them over her lips. The slight light from the moon breaking through shows the glistening shine that is left behind.

Fallon takes a deep breath in before I pull back. Staying completely still, my eyes focus on her face, watching for further signs of life. It's about to get good. She can't fucking wake up now.

Confident she is still out, I grab my cock and line it up with the perfect hole I've cut in her shorts. With careful movements, I begin to push the tip inside her.

Her wetness helping to ease me in. This is the first time she has allowed entry of my giant cock without any resistance. I fucking knew she wanted it, but her stupid little head fought her body. Until now.

Her pussy sucks my cock in, gripping it just like I had anticipated.

The further I thrust in, the lower I have to position my body. My hands are now on either side of her torso. Her legs are spread, allowing me room to position myself comfortably over her. Another moan—louder this time—leaves her mouth. Her head falls to the side and her hand moves to her clit, working herself as my cock continues to be sucked into her vise.

"Merrick," grumbles out of her mouth. My eyes dart up to her face, but her eyes remain closed.

Slowly fucking her, I brush my lips against her, tasting her arousal, and my tastebuds ignite. I didn't think I could taste anything anymore. Her evil cunt tastes like it should be forbidden. It's a weapon used to tempt us bad boys, only to poison us afterward. If that's what she was sent here for, then I would gladly let her take me down.

My tongue reaches out for one more taste. One more hit of her sweet release.

I am lost in that frenzy. Only her pussy gripping

my dick brings me back. My desperate little slut begs for my cock, even in her sleep. Her breath is warm against my face as she begins to milk me, and my name leaves her mouth once more.

I slam into her once more as my orgasm takes over. It's more intense than when I was alive. My entire body feels like it's floating as ropes of my warm cum empty into her. Filling her up with each buck of my hips. I couldn't fucking care if she woke up right now.

She raises her hands to the headboard behind her. Stabilizing herself while we both cum. Fallon's eyes are still closed. This girl must think she is having the best fucking dream.

As my frenzy dies down, so do my movements. My cock pounds into her one more time as the final bit of cum leaves my balls.

Pulling out slowly, her own release is mixed with mine and I'm sure we are both dripping out of her. Using my arms, I push myself up onto my knees. Looking down long enough to tuck myself back in and zip myself up. I glance back up, and her eyes are wide open, her hands covering her mouth,

"Ah, my desperate little slut is awake. Too bad you missed the main performance. It was like a fucking slip and slide this time." I casually tell her.

"Your desperate little slut?" Her words are muffled by her hands still covering her mouth.

"You picked up on that quickly. It's something new I'm trying." I respond, getting up from the mattress to stand at the foot of her bed.

She doesn't speak. Instead, she lifts her hands and brushes her fingers past her nose, sniffing. Her body swiftly moves, and Fallon sits up on the bed, pressing her body back to the headboard. She brings her knees up and wraps her arms around them. "What the fuck did you do? ANSWER ME!" So fucking dramatic.

Raking my fingers through my hair, "I think it's pretty obvious, stupid little girl."

Fallon brings one hand under her bent legs, then looks at it, covered in our combined release. "You motherfucker!" I cut her off and point at her. "We have been over this several times now. I have never fucked Joanie. How many times do you need to be told this?" My dick would voluntarily shrivel up and fall off if it ever got anywhere near Joanie's diseased waffle.

"I don't fucking care if you have or haven't fucked her. You are an asshole. You're truly a vile and sad excuse of whatever the fuck you are. You fucked me while I was sleeping. You never had consent. You forced your ghost dick inside of me when I never wanted it!" She is getting shouty now. Annoying and shouty.

I don't do the moaning and groaning, and I fire back at her, "Do you have a point? Also, your cunt very much wanted me this time. She was dripping wet. I painted some on your lips, they looked dry."

Muttering under her breath, "Fucking unbelievable. You are something else, Merrick. Such a prick." Then she gets shouty again. "Don't you get that this was wrong? You are wrong!"

"You're slightly overreacting. You never want it when you're awake. What else was I supposed to do?" I hold my arms out. What does she want from me?

Don't fuck her while awake, she says. Don't fuck her in her sleep, she says.

Then when am I supposed to do it?

Darla's advice is complete bullshit. This did not fix anything.

Dropping my arms down, and throwing my head back, I talk to the ceiling. "Darla said to make it better. To fix it. So, giving you a good fuck was my fixing things. I know how mad you get when I fuck you when you're awake, so, this seemed like the only obvious solution." Looking back down, she looks completely confused. Which part is confusing? It all seems to make sense to me.

Fuck my life. Oh, that's right, I'm a fucking ghost. My life was fucked, before I fixed it.

"Merrick. You are completely delusional. You know that, right? This behavior isn't normal."

Every ounce of me wants to bite back. She is delusional if she thinks she didn't love every moment of my cock pounding into her cunt just now. But all I hear is Darla's voice, telling me to fix it.

Nope. Fuck it.

"Your cunt begged for me. You moaned my name —twice! You want it as much as I do. Accept it. It's happening again. It's going to happen as many times as possible. Now stop acting like a stupid little girl. When we both know you are a desperate little slut."

Nothing. She only sits there staring at me.

"I can still see our cum dripping out of you. Now be a good little slut and open your legs so I can lick you clean." I demand while walking forward to the bed again, climbing on it and crawling the short distance to her.

Raising my eyebrows at her, "Open them. Now. Don't make me slap her for being naughty."

Fallon still doesn't speak, but she does listen. Good fucking girl. She is learning.

Her legs fall open to either side. She is still resting against the headboard, and I can see her pussy perfectly through cuts I made in her shorts.

Dipping my head down, my tongue peaks out as I lick up her folds. The taste of her sweet release mixed with mine erupts on my tongue. It's so fucking good.

Going back in for more, I continue collecting both our releases in my mouth. Allowing it to sit on my tongue before swallowing each time. Her fingers grab hold of my hair, pushing me back down to finish the job. Flicking her sensitive clit, Fallon's hips buck against my face. My tongue continues circling it, and she uses my face to chase her orgasm.

"Keep doing that. It's coming. I'm cumming," she moans.

Her cunt is still sensitive from earlier.

Cum drips out of her pussy as her orgasm hits, and I continue lapping it into my mouth. Fallon rubs herself against me once more before letting go of my hair. Licking her clean, I raise my head. Feeling her release dripping down my chin. The need for it to dry against my skin is strong, so I don't make an effort to clean it.

Instead, I look up at her. "See, it wasn't so bad just giving into it, now was it?"

Fallon pushes my head back. "Get out of my room."

Chuckling at her as I rise from the bed, I give her a wink that I'm not sure she can see in the dark. Before disappearing, I taunt her once more because nothing gets my dick harder than messing with Fallon.

"Until next time, stupid little girl."

CHAPTER 21
FALLON

The full moon is approaching, only a couple of days away. I am sitting in a cemetery in the middle of the cold night, trying to make friends with the spirits that live here.

Merrick has been missing in action since the other night. Which can only mean one thing, that he is up to no good.

Probably plotting his next attack on me. One minute he is doing it to try and make me regret my life, the next he is genuinely enjoying himself while I'm asleep.

But he isn't my priority.

Let him float about, and I will deal with him whenever he pops up again.

Now that cunt, Joanie. If she's noticed the goblet

missing, she hasn't said anything. It's only because she thinks I don't know anything. That or out of fear that a reaction could tip me off. Or she actually has no idea.

Fuck, she is going to be a terror if she finds out I have it, and that I know everything about the legacy of the town and our family. We only need to make it a couple more days.

I've gone through everything we found in the attic, which was the same day Merrick hung her over the balcony.

I found pictures of my dad as a kid and they brought tears to my eyes. He looked happy and innocent. Free of the burdens of being an adult.

There were a few photos of him and Merrick being happy kids. Playing in the yard or riding their bikes on the driveway.

There was also a picture of their dad, and both boys look just like him. Dark eyes, and a sharp jawline. The smirk on the right side of their mouth raised. All three of them have it. And now all three of them are gone. Even thinking about the photo brings emotion to my eyes.

I wish I had more time with dad. I wasn't ready yet.

But it has also taught me so much, being thrown into the lion's den of adulting and Port Canyon.

If my grandfather was anything like my dad, I would have loved to get to know him. He hasn't appeared here yet. I wonder if he ever does? If he and Merrick still see each other? I hope so, I'd do anything to see mine again.

Then there's Merrick. He is one of a fucking kind.

It's like this entire situation is like a reality show and he is the host.

The more drama, the more entertainment and the more wildly inappropriate shit that comes out of his mouth, the happier he is.

He gets off on this shit.

Case in point, his dick got hard humiliating Joanie. That whole situation would have given him his highest rated episode.

Chuckling to myself at the thought, I catch myself smiling as well.

Thoughts of Merrick are making me smile? Jesus Christ, he must never know. His head would explode from massive ego syndrome.

Imagine if he knew that I enjoyed what he did the other night, as shocking as it was. Waking up, thinking I just had the most intense sex dream, only to find out it was real. Then he eats me out. First Class servicing.

Could ghosts come back from the dead twice? He would be so excited. Surely he would stroke out or have a heart attack or something?

I've always liked the idea of waking up to someone fucking me.

It's like, you know how guys dream of waking up to a blowjob?

For guys, it doesn't always come with the same feeling. For me, it means they truly love you if they want to be inside of you, even when you're asleep.

Like you're an addiction.

Fuck, I'm explaining this terribly.

Oh, nope. Merrick does this. Not me. We will keep him talking to you guys.

This is his reality show, after all. We are just living in it.

I'm happy he isn't like Joanie, same with dad.

And in a couple of nights, her life will be in my hands.

Blood for Blood.

I've tried to imagine what it will be like. The entire experience. But I still can't wrap my mind around it. It doesn't seem real, yet.

The responsibility weighs heavier on me each day.

I need to do the legacy proud. Joanie tarnished it. I have to bring it back. Make it better.

So here I am, sitting outside in a graveyard that is located in my backyard. It's enormous, extending for acres in either direction. Once Joanie is relieved of her duties, it will give me more of an opportunity to explore it. To visit the rows upon rows of headstones, I wonder if there are more statues or crypts for other founding families.

I haven't found much on the other families. But the history, this life, it has grown on me. It's becoming more important to me to learn about it.

This is enough thinking for one night.

Turning my brain off, I focus on my surroundings. Being present in this moment.

It could be one of my last like this while I learn my new role.

Focusing on the sounds. On the tiny lives around me.

Crickets are chirping. Moths fly around the brightly lit lamps. The air is crisp in my lungs.

Harper was right, it is kind of perfect out here.

CHAPTER 22
FALLON
FULL MOON - SEPTEMBER 29

This is surreal.

This night, the last full moon before October, will be part of our town's history. The other founding families will gather to discuss this night for years to come. And maybe, one day, my own will as well.

There is no running away.

Even if my dad was able to leave, I still believe in the curse. The town let him think he was safe until it decided it was time to come back.

He died.

I found Joanie's number in his phone.

And now he has returned and so have I.

There was a moment, in the back of my head, where I had wanted to leave.

To get away from Port Canyon and never look back, but the pull to stay was stronger.

My internal drive to prove everyone wrong was stronger.

Merrick wanted to chase me. Torture me. Ruin me.

But it feels like I am the one ruining him.

And together, like it or not, we will ruin Joanie.

The thought makes my lips curve up. It's satisfying. I have gotten under his skin perfectly and I couldn't be more proud of myself for accomplishing that feat.

Joanie has pissed me off enough that murdering her doesn't seem so bad. I'm strangely excited about it all.

To have a purpose again. To have a family legacy. It makes me proud to be given this opportunity to uphold it and pass it down.

I'm standing in the bathroom, naked, looking in the mirror, taking it all in. Burning each moment of the evening into my brain. I want to remember every detail.

It's going to go by so fast.

My hair is down, with loose curls hanging down my back over my shoulders. A black, beaded headpiece sits on the crown of my head, and there's a single black jewel hanging down, resting on the middle of my forehead; matching black chandelier earrings completing the look. I found it all in a box in the attic, and with the dress Harper has been making, it felt like it would work perfectly. To be fair, what I have been picturing in my head could be completely off. She hasn't shown me or given any hints of what she's been up to. I know nothing other than the corset we found.

My makeup is minimal. Smokey eye and a nude lip. Some blush on my cheeks helps my fair skin pop.

"Fallon, I'm here." Harper announces her arrival and brings me back to reality.

"I'll be right out!" I take myself in once last time. "You got this. You were made for this." A chill sweeps across my skin, and goosebumps immediately appear.

It only means one thing.

Turning around, I don't bother covering myself. He has seen me like this awake and asleep; the man doesn't have any fucking boundaries.

He doesn't show himself at first. Looking around the large bathroom, where did he go?

Tonight is not the night for his games. My nerves are shot, and even though I feel confident, I am still taking a life. Blood for Blood.

Walking towards the closed bathroom door, I am about to open it when Merrick pops up in front of me. I jump, but he grabs my shoulders to keep me in place. It all happens so fast. He leans in and kisses me, and his lips are cold against mine. My eyes remain open in shock. Am I shocked? It's not like he's ever asked for permission before. Merrick takes what he wants, even if you don't want to give it to him.

Moving his hands from my shoulder, his fingers brush against my neck slowly. Once they reach my jawline, he grips my face and forces the kiss deeper. His tongue pushes past my lips and I let him in. Closing my eyes, my tongue brushes against his and a jolt of electricity spreads throughout my body. I bring my hands up to his forearms and hold on to him.

There is no point in fighting it. Merrick loves the battle, the struggle; it would only turn him on more.

We stay like this for a few moments. The longer we stay connected, the more it feels like he is sucking all the oxygen from my lungs. Even though I know he doesn't breathe.

The feeling is intense.

Before I know it, he is letting go of my face and he slowly breaks our connection. Stepping back, Merrick looks down at me. I keep my focus on him through my lashes. His pupils are dilated, and his white hair is disheveled over his forehead.

Biting my bottom lip, I whisper, "You kissed me… and you weren't an asshole about it."

He chuckles at my statement, wiping his lip with his thumb, then putting it in his mouth. Sucking on it before removing it to respond, "Yeah, I did. Plus, you're awake. Impressed?"

Breaking my focus on him, I roll my eyes.

"Merrick, I don't have time for your shit right now. Tomorrow, sure. But not tonight. Please, not tonight."

"Ah, my desperate little girl, you always have time for my shit. You love my shit. I pop up and adrenaline courses through your veins. The beating of your heart increases. You. Are. Addicted."

He never listens to me. The one time I need him to focus and listen, he can't be bothered.

"I'll tell you one thing that you don't know about me. Joanie doesn't even know about me."

Not moving, I wait for him to continue.

"I have a PhD." That's all he says. He doesn't elaborate.

Merrick seems to have forgotten I know he died when he was twenty. There's no chance he has a PhD unless he was a genius and I doubt that very much.

"Go on then," time is ticking.

He leans in again, his lips brush against my ear and he whispers, "I do. I know you're questioning it. Wondering how it is possible. But it is. If you think hard about it, you actually already know.... I have a Pretty Huge Dick. And he is standing at attention, for you and only you."

I can't help myself and laughter erupts from my chest.

Merrick steps back with the biggest smile on his face and grabs his cock through his jeans while moving his eyebrows at me.

Still laughing, I try to speak. "Out, Merrick. Go change and let me get ready in peace, please. Harper is here, waiting in my room." I shoo him away with my hands. He looks back at me, puzzled. "Wait. You think I choose to wear the same clothes every day? That I have the option to wear something else, but think '*Nah, I'm good*'? This is my only outfit, stupid little girl."

Anything is possible, but I don't have time to learn more about ghost logistics tonight.

My laughter has stopped and I'm looking at him with no expression.

Merrick bows at me. "Yes, as you wish." As he rises, he slaps one of my breasts and disappears.

Such an asshole.

Rushing out of the bathroom back to my room, "Shit. Sorry, Harper. I'm here."

Harper is sitting on the edge of my bed with a grin on her face, and a garment bag laid out next to her.

"Thin walls," is all she says back. Internally, I'm thankful she doesn't press. I want to tell her all about it, but we don't have time to gossip right now. We have a grandmother to kill and a legacy to take over. I check my phone, it's almost time.

Earlier today, Darla asked Joanie to come back this evening, as a few of the newer spirits wanted to meet with her. They were still feeling uneasy in their new life and needed guidance.

Joanie, naturally, salivated at the idea. She gets off on this shit. Thinking one of the spirits really needs her after keeping away from her for years.

Harper and her dad alerted the other founding family elders discreetly, and they will be in the grave-yard, out of sight, waiting for the time.

Joanie still hasn't accused me of taking the goblet. She must have had it somewhere out of view. Hidden away. It's the only explanation at this point and I will take it. The less she knows, the easier this will be for us to execute.

Literally and figuratively.

I scrunch my nose. Did I just make a pun about execution?

The asshole is rubbing off on me.

Disgusting.

"Earth to Fallon." Harper is waving her hand in front of my face.

"Yes. Sorry I'm here. It's just a lot. I'm ready. Right?"

She turns around to the garment bag and begins unzipping it. "You were made for this."

I was. I am.

We both were. Soon it will be my best friend's turn.

Tears well in my eyes as she turns around again. "No. Not today. You can cry tomorrow. Tonight, your makeup looks too good to ruin. So, stop it. Right now, and let's get you dressed!" She scolds me.

"You are so adorable when you get all firm with me, you know that?" Her eyes widen and she retorts. "He is rubbing off on you. I'm not sure how I feel about this, but I know I'm adorable, thank you."

Shaking my head while laughing at her, I walk toward her and fully open the garment bag. My jaw drops, on top is the corset on its own royal purple silk hanger, but it's what's underneath that takes my breath away.

It's black see through lace with black butterflies and a floral design embroidered into it. As I stare at the masterpiece, Harper takes the corset off the hanger. "Here, put this on first." She instructs while passing it to me. Bringing my attention back, I take the delicate piece from her and begin putting it on. Putting my legs through the opening, and pulling it up my body, I place the straps over my shoulders. Harper begins doing up the back for me. Running my hands along the fabric, admiring the sweetheart neckline, and I'm so pleased it fits my frame perfectly.

"Ok, this next piece is delicate. One snag on a hangnail and it's ruined. So be very careful." Harper scolds me while bringing out the lace, looking at it in the bag I wasn't sure how it would work. Seeing it now, she sewed me an entire dress. It's stunning.

She is holding it open for me, squatted on the ground so I can step in. Once I step in, Harper slowly starts to rise with it, moving it up my body. All I want to do is touch it and admire her masterpiece.

"Arms in the openings," she whispers.

We are having a moment, and I am fully living in it.

It's soft against my skin. Not rough like I thought it would be. The sleeves are long and form perfectly against my arms.

Harper moves around me to maneuver the rest of it up and over my shoulders. The neckline wraps around my throat, and there's a zipper up the back.

Turning to the mirror, I take myself in.

The dress is form-fitting from the waist up, and the corset shows perfectly through the black lace. The sporadic, but perfectly placed, embroidered flowers and butterflies are on full display as it flows down from the fitted waist. It's been tailored for my height, and leaves a short train running behind me. It's stunning.

I'm speechless.

"How can I ever repay you? Harper, this is... I have no words."

"Just say thank you. That's all I need."

Turning around carefully to face her, I'm still lost for words and all I can say is, "Thank you."

She fixes my hair, making some of it fall back over my shoulders.

I look at her through the mirror's reflection, still amazed. "How did you know my measurements? It fits perfectly, Harper. You are so talented."

Harper looks down at her feet before looking back up at me, hesitantly, "My mom. She has a similar frame and build to you. So I used her."

I've never seen or heard her really speak about her mom before.

"Your mom. Is she around? You have never mentioned her to me before."

Biting her lip and shifting her eyes slightly. "My mom… my mom died a few years ago."

"Shit, I'm sorry Harper. I had no idea. Will we see her tonight at the ceremony?"

She shakes her head slightly. "No. She isn't buried here yet. You see… My dad… We have kept her preserved, and she's still at home with us. It's been hard on dad. She was his life. I help him keep her how she is. To the best of our ability."

I wrap her in a hug. She needs to know I would never judge her or her family for that. I'm about to end the life of Joanie, even if I wanted to judge, I couldn't.

Stepping back after a few moments, Harper gives me a slight smile. "I'll meet you out there. You got this. You were born for this." She kisses my cheek before leaving the room and closing the door behind her.

I continue to admire this dress, and notice a black box on the bed. Holding my dress up, I walk to the bed and open it. Inside are black sandal stiletto heels.

Feeling the familiar chill, Merrick pops up next to me.

Without saying a word, he grabs one shoe and bends to the floor with it. Carefully, he moves the fabric to show my bare foot. Placing the shoe to the ground, he gently takes my foot and guides it in. His fingers bush against the calf of my leg, and a chill runs up my spine. Once my foot is fully in the shoe, he takes the strap at the ankle and does it up.

I pass him the second shoe, and he does the same thing. This is the most intimate moment we have ever had.

Before getting up, he takes one shoe-clad foot in his hand, raising it slightly and kisses the top of my foot before putting it back to the ground.

"Don't worry, I haven't gone soft on you. I'll have you on your knees licking my shoes and balls later." Merrick says looking up at me with a wink.

Fucking asshole.

I just shake my head. Merrick will be Merrick, there is no changing it.

"I need to bring the goblet and dad with me. Can you help me with that?" I ask, without acknowledging his remark.

Standing up, he brushes my cheek with this thumb. "The goblet and blade are in the crypt already.

I moved it after Joanie finished there this afternoon. Everyone is already down there, waiting in the shadows. Before coming here, I saw Joanie starting her walk back out through my bedroom window. So grab your dad. The rest is already waiting for you."

Looking at him puzzled, "Your room?"

"Yeah, it's across the hall."

All this time, he was across the hall from me? "But when I went exploring one day, that door was locked."

"Joanie locked it after I died. I don't need a key to get in. I'm a ghost. Remember?"

"Of course I remember. I was just, never mind."

"You're nervous, but you don't need to be. We are all here with you."

And just like that, he's gone.

Taking one more deep breath, I walk towards the shelving and pick up my dad.

"Ok, Daddy. The one thing you tried to protect me from. That you tried to escape. Is now the one thing I know I was meant to do. I love you and thank you for being my dad." I kiss the urn.

The only thing that would complete this night is if he were here with me.

CHAPTER 23
FALLON

The night is foggy. It slithers on top of the ground and covers my feet. The sky is clear as the moon shines down Port Canyon. I pass the Angel of Death and realize she makes sense being here now. Unlike on my first day, she is absolutely beautiful tonight.

She knows the torch is about to go out for another soon.

Garden lights surround her amongst the flowers and they light the pathway to the gated archway within the hedges. As soon as I open that gate, my old life will be left behind. Walking along the stone walkway, my heels click against them with each stride.

The evening chill causes goosebumps to rise along my arms. It's a different energy out here than most nights. I can feel it in my bones, and my stomach is uneasy. Every part of me hopes Joanie hasn't caught on. That she went willingly to the mausoleum, unknowingly maneuvering her own demise. Whether she saw it this way is irrelevant. Her overbearing attitude that the dead are indebted to her is what has led to this. She was meant to protect them, help them, and take care of spirits, new and old. Not act as though they would be stranded without her.

With one arm wrapped around dad, I move to open the gate, but something doesn't feel right. Stopping mid-reach, I pull my arm back.

"Merrick. Can you help me, please?" I could feel him with me during my walk here.

He pops up, back leaning against the gate all cool and casual, "You rang?"

Rolling my eyes, "I did. Thank you. Can you help take my shoes off? I want to feel the earth beneath my feet when I enter the cemetery. It will make me feel more connected to them."

Merrick smirks at me, shaking his head as he bends down, "Chicks are fucking weird."

Slightly lifting the front of my dress to expose my foot. Brushing his fingers up my calf before unbuckling the strap and gently sliding the shoe off my foot.

He does the same with my other shoe. "I'm keeping these."

Looking down at him, confused, but I don't argue. They are horribly uncomfortable. "Go for it. I don't need them."

He stands with my shoes in hand and chuckles at me. "Oh, my desperate little slut, I'll have you in them naked while riding my cock later, don't you worry." Merrick taps the urn with his finger, "Don't worry brother, I'll take good care of your little girl. She likes it rough, so don't mind the handprints decorating her body once I'm done."

"Shut up!" I hiss at him while glaring.

Merrick throws the shoes off into the hedges. "I'll be back for those later." Then grabs my throat and devours my lips with his mouth. The kiss is quick, but rough; hard and passionate. Like all the air is being sucked out of me. His strong hand squeezes a bit tighter before releasing me and stepping back.

"Are you ready to take what's yours?" He asks, looking down at me with a raised eyebrow.

"I am."

"Good. Now let's go. Everyone is waiting and Joanie is already bitching about being out there so late. She still has no idea. She won't until you make it known." Merrick explains while opening the gate in front of us.

"Stay with me?"

Turning around again with a sinister smile displayed brightly on his face, "I wouldn't miss this for the fucking world. So let's get moving. The clock is ticking. Your people—your spirits—are waiting, m'lady."

He opens the gate, and I begin to walk through the archway. My bare feet guide me down the candle lit pathway to the cemetery. The earth and stone beneath my bare feet feels more natural as the train to my dress slides behind me with each step. When the gate closes, the latch clicks, and I can hear Merrick's footsteps behind me.

Looking around, there crows are sitting on the branches above me, a couple caw as I pass.

As we approach the cemetery opening, I can faintly hear Joanie, "I'm done playing your fucking games. Next time you need something, I won't come running. Then who will help your asses?"

There will never be a next time, old lady.

"Hey, look behind you," Merrick whispers softly in my ear. Turning my head slightly to either side, I see spirits and the elders behind me, including Harper and her dad. She gives me a quick reassuring smile before I refocus on what is ahead of me.

Emotion builds in my chest and the moment feels more real than it did even minutes ago. This is more significant than I think I had realized.

Fog rises in the cemetery, and a gust of wind blows in, rustling the leaves on the trees. A hand clasps mine, bringing me back to the moment.

"Stay here for a minute, stupid little girl." Merrick instructs.

I don't argue it.

Holding my dad tighter. Pulling from his strength to help me through this.

As we wait, I can feel my heart beating inside my chest. The anticipation is half the battle. The other is actually following through with what they have asked of me.

To kill. To murder, Joanie.

My eyes shift around, trying to catch a glimpse of whatever is happening within the fog in front of us. The surrounding silence is eerie, and the visibility is zero. No matter how hard I focus, I see and hear nothing.

"Merrick. What's happening?" I question just loud enough so he can hear me.

His lips brush against my hair. "Shh, just wait."

He doesn't add a smartass comment at the end. It's the most serious he has ever been around me. Which makes me uncomfortable. We aren't serious. We are sarcastic and stubborn.

Never serious.

I'm in my own head now. The waiting makes it harder to stay in the present. My mind wants to wander, to make up stories of what might be happening beyond cemetery entrance.

Before I can get too lost in my own thoughts, the fog begins to lift.

The Angel of Mercy is the first thing I see. Ready to receive a blessing on behalf of the deceased with her hands open on bent knees.

"It's time," Merrick whispers, breaking me from my spell. I nod, not saying a word. Instead, I put one foot in front of the other.

As more of the fog lifts, and the space is empty where Joanie once stood.

"Where is she?"

"Stupid little girl, go to the mausoleum. Everything is how it is meant to be," Merrick reassures me.

Turning my head slightly, I am comforted when I find the elders and their families behind me.

The spirits are gone. The candles that once lit along the pathway are out.

I retrain my focus on what's in front of me.

Walking over the threshold into the cemetery, the crows have left their perch and are flying above us. A few are still perched on tombstones, curiously observing us as we move toward our goal. The energy has changed. Strength and confidence engulf me.

This is my moment. My time. My legacy.

My pace rapidly increases once I catch sight of my family's mausoleum. Torches are lit at the entrance, the fire flickering in the dark of night, reflecting off the stone walls. It reminds of the Angel of Death in the backyard. Except for her torch is no longer burning. It all feels very symbolic.

Once Joanie has been dealt with and her torch extinguished, she will plead for mercy, but it will not come for her.

I am guided to the entrance. It is time.

Merrick steps in front of me and opens the iron door. He enters first, holding the door open for me.

With my dad still in my arms, I bring him inside. There are lanterns hung, which light the space for us. I walk past Merrick and enter the large enclosed space, and see stone shelving on the wall immediately in front of me. Something comes over me and without hesitating, I know I need to place my dad there. Using both hands, I place his urn on the middle shelf so he is front and center.

"You evil bitch!"

Joanie's scream throws me off. It's not something I expected. Turning to the right, I take in the scene in front of me.

Multiple spirits, including Darla, are holding her down against a cold concrete slab that is elevated by an above-ground casket.

The sound of the iron door closing startles me from taking everything in.

Merrick wastes no time and joins the other spirits. He grabs hold of Joanie's face and looks her right in the eye. "It's show time."

CHAPTER 24

MERRICK

"Ladies and Gentlemen. Boys and Girls. Welcome to the main fucking event!"

If this was a circus, I'd be your ringmaster.

But this! This is so much fucking better than a circus.

This is everything I have been waiting for, since that night I drove off the bridge.

Letting go of Joanie's leathery face, I step back like a giddy fucking school boy who just jerked off for the first time into a sock. The soft, warm fabric wrapped around my cock while I jerked my hand up and down my shaft. After cumming in it, I'd throw it in the hamper for Joanie to wash.

Thinking back to it, and knowing that Joanie would clean up my dirty cum filled sock almost makes me just as giddy. But enough about me and my cock—for now. My desperate little slut must focus on the ceremony first.

"Joanie—mother of the fucking year—what a predicament you seem to find yourself in. If only I cared enough to help you. Too bad I don't." Taunting her as I slap her face a couple times for good measure.

"What a disappointment. You. Your brother. Your father. I'm glad the three of you died. It's what you deserved. Another breath wasted on any of you three would be one too many." The bitch has a bite.

"Merrick, stop playing with my dinner." Fuck me. I think I just came in my pants. Biting down on my fist as I turn to where the sweet angel sang to me. Fallon has never been as fucking hot as she is now. Her eyes tell me she knows exactly what she's done to me. They scream mischief. With a cheeky smirk and hands on her hips.

Fallon exudes confidence. This is her element. She belongs here. If ever there was a doubt in my mind, it is gone. Dammit, I'll have to find new and exciting ways to torture her for my pleasure. Walking up to my little slut, taking her all in, she is so fucking powerful. I place my hand around her neck as I circle to stand behind her.

Still holding her throat, I reach my other arm out and shout, "Harper! The blade." My voice echoes, bouncing off the walls.

She was meant to be by the door, waiting. What in the fuck is taking her so long?

"Harper!"

"Fuck off, Merrick. I'm coming. This door is fucking heavy, you know." Such a child.

It is slowly pushed open, and I see her dad helping her as she slips in with the blade in hand.

My arm is still reaching out in front of her now. Wiggling my fingers in her face, she gets the hint and places the silver blade with a black leather handle into my hand. We agreed she would stay for this. To support Fallon.

This ghost has a heart, after all. Does that scare you? It should. It scares the shit out of me, if I think about it for too long.

Harper steps back behind us, out of the way. Now we need the goblet.

"Mark! The goblet." Fallon's eyes widened in shock.

That's right, little girl, daddy's home.

FALLON

Trembling hands cover my mouth in shock. Tears well in my eyes.

My dad is here, standing in front of me. He looks like he did before he died. The same short dark hair, stubble lining his jaw, bushy eyebrows and that smirk that I know now runs in the family. He is wearing his classic dad blue jeans, white trainers and black polo shirt. In his hand, he is holding the goblet, the exact one that Merrick stole out of Joanie's room.

"Daddy," I whimper. He takes a step forward. "Hi, baby girl."

I try to move forward, but Merrick squeezes my throat tighter. "Focus." He snarks in my ear.

Slowly nodding at his statement, he continues, "Family reunion later. You need to focus."

"Ok. Yeah." Agreeing with him, but tears still stream down my face from the shock. I've missed my dad so much.

"The more you cry, the harder I get." Merrick whispers behind me while rubbing his erection into my backside.

"He is right, baby girl. This is your time. You

need to focus. I'll be here by your side the entire time." Dad reassures me as he walks to stand next to me, facing Joanie.

Lowering my hands from my face, Merrick brings the blade up to my chest. Using the sharp tip, he brushes it lightly across my collarbone. It doesn't break skin, but one accidental move from me and it could.

"All the ingrates are here now. While I'm being held down by cowards. Fucking degenerates of the afterlife. None of you are worthy. You will fail. You will ruin this family and the name I have built."

"Shut up. I've had enough of you. You open your damn mouth and bullshit spews out of it. You have been nasty since I got here, but apparently, that's just the way you are. If anyone isn't worthy, it's you. You are not worthy of this family. Of this privileged life that was gifted to you. You had your chance to succeed, to be a good person, but it's not in you. You were born nasty and you will die nasty." Not wanting to stoop even further to her level, I bite my tongue. Then I grab Merrick's hand, which is still caressing my bare skin.

"Ah, my stupid little girl might not be stupid any longer," he says to me skeptically.

He places the blade into my hand and lets go of

my throat.

There is no going back now.

CHAPTER 25
FALLON

Darla and I make eye contact.

It's time.

"Boys, please join me and form a circle around Joanie. Mark, bring the goblet. Harper. You can stay. You are the next legacy to have this ceremony… but with a little less death. It's good for you to see the process."

"Look at Darla over here with the jokes," Merrick sounds impressed. He never sounds impressed.

"I'm more than just an elder spirit." She bites back with a wink.

My dad moves to stand at Joanie's head and Merrick, while rubbing his hands together, stands next to her torso in front of me.

All eyes are on me. My heart is racing.

Darla begins to whisper, "May the elders bless this sacred ceremony. May they bless Fallon and give her the strength to fulfill her responsibilities that the founding families have gifted her. Blood for Blood."

Joanie struggles against the hold they have on her. No matter how hard she fights, it's pointless. Her fate has been written.

Hearing Darla's request to bless this ceremony has reassured me. This is what I must do, and with dad, Merrick, and Harper by my side, I have renewed confidence. Joanie would have never let go. She would have only suffocated the spirits further with her mistreatment. She was given this. The town trusted her, and she's destroyed her legacy.

Joanie knows the rules.

My bare feet slap against the cold floor with each step forward.

"Are you sure you are your dad's daughter? Your mom was a whore. This could all be for nothing. Then what? You ungrateful vermin will have no one, then you will fade away. Nothing but forgotten spirits, lost and alone." Desperate, Joanie is grasping at anything. She is nothing but a nasty old lady who is about to have it all taken from her. These are only hurtful words to buy her time. I'm too much like my dad to not be blood.

"Would you please shut the fuck up? You. Are. Done. You became obsessed with this fucking place. To the point that you've made everyone around you miserable, including yourself. You think people owe you. You gave up your family to fulfill your duties, which no one asked you to do. You took it too fucking far. And now, instead of having a civilized, peaceful transition, this has to happen. You did this. All of it. Including dad, Mark, and me. This is all on fucking you." Merrick spits back at her. As big as this is for me, he has years of built up anger toward her. This is just as important to him, if not more so. I wait while he lets it all out. Respecting his final moments with her.

Not wanting to make this about me, because I am only one part of this, though I wonder if he will resent me for taking over one day.

"Get out of your head, little girl. It won't be the same," Merrick whispers to me. I nod my head slightly, acknowledging that I hear him. I believe him.

He continues his verbal assault on Joanie. "No other family has had this fucking problem. Do you see that? Do you fucking get it?" He taps the side of his own head.

Merrick shows us his confident side, his ego and his 'I don't give a fuck attitude', but deep down, he is hurting. It makes me sad for him and my dad.

We all had mom's who didn't care or prioritize us.

"Oh, enough of you, boy. It was a lot more peaceful around here when you weren't." I've had enough of this old bitch.

Only I get to be a dick to Merrick.

My hand is shaking when I lift the blade and press it against her arm being held above her head, and blood trickles behind it. The cut is shallow, a scrape really. Just a test to see if I could do it.

I can.

Out of the corner of my eye, I see Merrick read-just himself. He is never not hard.

It is slightly embarrassing now that dad is here. But that is really the least of my worries at the moment.

"Pussy. Knew you couldn't do it." Joanie mumbles.

Merrick inches closer to me, feeling his presence against my skin, I feed off his strength and continue. I move the blade from her arm up to her face and gingerly glide it down. I stop thinking, letting my body take over and do what feels natural. Stopping at her throat, I take the tip and slowly begin taunting her.

This is more fun than I anticipated, and a smile forms on my lips.

"It isn't nice to play with your food, stupid little girl," Merrick whispers in my ear, and I bite my bottom lip. "Do it, ear to ear."

Bringing the pointed edge to below the ear that is furthest away from me, I push it in. It must hurt because her body reacts.

"You're getting off on this, aren't you? I can smell your desperate pussy from here."

I move the blade slowly under her jawline, and watch as the skin parts beneath the blade and a stream of red follows.

"Your cunt is dripping for me, isn't it?"

Shifting my eyes to Merrick, he winks at me and motions his head for me to continue.

"Does my desperate little slut like it when I come in her mouth? Choking on my cock? You like being my whore, little girl?"

Swallowing the saliva that builds up in my mouth at the thought of choking on his cock. My mouth continues to water as the blade cuts through Joanie's skin. Before reaching the front of her throat, I pull the blade out and begin to cut from her ear closest to me. Not wanting to finish her off just yet.

"If I asked you to stick your fingers up your pussy

right here, in front of everyone, would you disobey me, slut? Or would you get off on it? I bet you would fucking love it."

My body is heating up, and the corset feels tighter with each breath.

Blood coats the silver blade and begins to stain the concrete slab that Joanie is being held on. It is no longer just a trickle of crimson red, it's flowing out faster with each cut. I press deeper and deeper, harder and harder.

"You want Joanie's blood coating your fingers while they slide in and out of your needy cunt, wishing it was my cock."

I place my free hand in the blood pooling at her side, finding it warm and thick.

"You are a fucking Queen. Nothing can stop you now."

With that final word of encouragement, I rapidly finish the cut. Slicing from ear to ear, joining the cuts, I go as deep as I possibly can with as much force as I can muster. I hope it's enough as I drop the blade to the ground next to me. I'm sure it makes a noise as it hits the floor, but I am too dazed to hear it.

I watch Joanie's eyes, needing to know what it is to take a life. Blood for Blood

"Not even Harper's dad will want to fuck your dead body. I'm going to let the crows eat your eyes and coyotes use you as their own personal shit bag after skull fucking your holes." Those are Merrick's final words to her as life leaves her body. Her eyes go from alert and bright to dull and dead. Just like that.

Blood is all over the floor, and my feet are covered in it. The warmth of it feels nice between my toes.

"Mark, give her the goblet." Darla instructs.

My dad passes me the silver chalice. Taking both hands, I wrap my fingers around it.

"Now fill it up, my child." Blood is flowing out of Joanie's neck and mouth. I collect the blood from her neck, filling the goblet to the top like Darla instructed.

"Fallon, repeat after me: My Legacy. My Legend. My Responsibility. I swear to protect the sacred space that our ancestors and fallen elders call home. To be their caregiver and provide sanctuary. Port Canyon, forever their home and mine. 'Til death and in the afterlife."

I do, word for word, while looking her in the eyes.

"My Legacy. My Legend. My Responsibility. I swear to protect the sacred space that our ancestors and fallen elders call home. To be their caregiver and provide sanctuary. Port Canyon, forever their home and mine…"

The energy in the room elevates and powerful forces surround us as a gust of what feels like wind weaves around me. My feet rise from the ground as I say the last line, "'Til death and in the afterlife."

"Now drink, my child. Drink until the last drop."

I already know it's going to be terrible when I place the goblet to my lips. Squeezing my eyes shut, I tip it back and begin pouring the contents into my mouth. The warm, coppery iron taste of blood touches my tongue. It coats my mouth and throat as I drink it. My gag reflex tries to stop me, but I force myself to keep going. The excess is running down my chin onto my chest. Breathing through my nose, I take another big gulp. '*Come on Fallon. Do this. You're almost done. Just finish it*' I keep telling myself. Lights are flashing around me as I open my eyes to find that I remain elevated off the floor. The goblet has one last sip left. Throwing it back, I drain it. Thick, warm blood coats my mouth and throat. It feels heavy in my stomach.

My arms spread as my head tilts up and I drop the goblet to the floor. A high-pitched scream leaves my mouth. Once what felt like slow motion, suddenly turns into warp speed.

Then it all just stops.
The wind is gone.
The lights go out.
My body falls to the floor.
Everything goes dark.

CHAPTER 26
MERRICK

The wicked bitch of the west is dead.

My brother isn't a bunch of dried up dust anymore.

My girl is fucking levitating.

Dreams do come true.

I watch in amazement. I'm pretty sure it was talking about her finger fucking herself with Joanie's blood that really brought this party to the next level like this.

The flames flicker around us. A different energy has entered the space. I've never heard of any other full moon ceremony like this. Fallon continues to drink from the goblet. Blood runs down her chin and coats her exposed chest. Droplets of crimson drip off her feet, back down to the puddle of it on the floor.

As the goblet falls from Fallon's hand and connects with the hard ground, it bounces a couple of times before rolling off. An ear aching high-pitched scream follows. My eyes beam over to Darla, what the fuck is happening? She responds by shaking her head; she's also in a state of disbelief. And then, as quickly as it all began, it stops.

Fallon's petite frame, covered in gorgeous black lace, falls to the floor. The flames go out and the room is completely silent.

"Merrick. What was that?" Harper's trembling voice questions. I'm frozen, unable to move or respond.

"Fallon, baby girl." My brother's voice is coming from the same direction as Fallon.

The noise of a match being lit catches my attention. Harper is relighting the lanterns.

Mark is kneeling next to Fallon's body, one of her tiny hands in his. She isn't moving.

"Darla!" I shout, my voice echoes in the room. Everyone looks up at me.

She moves from behind the slab where Joanie lays dead, over to Fallon and Mark. My eyes follow her. Harper waits, her face filled with fear.

So is mine.

Darla bends down and touches Fallon's forehead,

and I can't read her face. Her hand moves to Fallon's exposed chest, and she starts whispering. Her lips are moving, but I can't make out what she's saying. Mark is watching Darla as closely as I am. She nods her head a couple times. Like she's communicating with someone or something. Then, looking over her shoulder, she looks at me. Locking eyes.

"She will be ok. She will be changed, but she will still be Fallon. She will wake up when she's ready. Merrick, will you take her back to the house? Let her rest. She is tired."

What the fuck is going on? Raking my hands through my hair, I try to understand what happened here tonight while absorbing what Darla's just said.

"Merrick, please. Harper, once Fallon is gone, can you grab your father? We will need help with Joanie's body. We can't have her coming back in spirit form. There are precautions we must take. We will need your help too, Mark."

My feet move before I realize it. Fallon's body is limp when I pick her up, bridal style, in my arms.

Harper races over and pulls open the door as quickly as she can. Adrenaline must be coursing through her, because that's a heavy fucking door that she struggled with before. Now it's like she's the fucking hulk.

The bright moon shines down as we step outside.

Ghosts and the elder families gather around. Gasps can be heard as they see who I'm carrying.

They part, clearing a path for me and as I speed past them with my stupid little girl, lifeless in my arms.

Fog still settles on the ground, not as thick as it was earlier, and I can see the light from the house in the distance. I pick up the pace when I see the gate to the backyard is still open. We can't get back to the house and her room fast enough. My feet move rapidly, passing the Angel of Death, "You took one today already, you don't get her too." Greedy bitch.

Rushing up the steps of the porch, the wooden floor creaks beneath me as my booted feet rush across them. I open the back door swiftly.

Continuing with my same pace, I make our way through the house and to the entrance way where the grand staircase resides.

I want to take the stairs two at a time, but with my luck, I'll eat shit and send Fallon flying. Then someone would pop up yelling karma or some shit.

Reaching the landing where the stairs separate the house into two wings, I look out the large window, but I'm unable to see anything past the hedges. Turning up to Fallon's wing, she still has not stirred.

Running down the long hallway, the door is open to her room. Not needing the light—I'm a fucking ghost —I reach her bed and place her down on it gently. I want to take her gown off, but I know Harper will kill me if I ruin it.

Popping quickly out of her room to mine, I grab the blanket off my bed and head back into her room. I drape the black duvet over her, to keep her warm and comfortable. Her head lies on her pillow with her long, dark hair framing her beautiful face. Seeing Joanie's dried blood on her face gets my cock hard again. Fuck bro, not now.

My cock wants to slide between her lips. Normally, Fallon being asleep wouldn't stop me, but I can't like this. Darla would fucking destroy me if she caught me or found out. The full moon ceremony isn't over until she wakes up, and I can't fuck any of it up.

Getting into bed next to her, I sit against her headboard and watch her. Watch her and wait. Hoping she wakes up soon.

She has to wake up.

CHAPTER 27
FALLON

My body is frozen.

My eyes won't open, and my lips won't move. After what feels like days, but could be hours, I can hear hushed words breaking through the silence.

My blanket smells like Merrick. I miss him. He rushed me back home so quickly. He's scared. I can feel it. When I hear him speak, he masks it.

I'm scared too. Why can't I wake up?

"Bro, Darla said not to touch anything, don't change anything. We can't risk shit."

My thoughts are interrupted by Merrick yelling at my dad. They want to clean my hands and face. Merrick is worried it could mess up whatever is happening.

As completely fucking insane as he is, he cares about me. He just shows it in strange ways.

"That's my kid laying there. Lifeless. I just got her fucking back. I can't lose her. I can't."

My dad sounds defeated. I'm not gone, dad. You won't lose me.

Ever.

"You're lucky I have been told to keep my hands off you, my desperate little slut. You have no idea how badly I want to fuck those perky tits of yours right now. We are keeping this corset."

Feeling his finger caress my chest, he gets closer and whispers, "Your dad caught me jerking off to you earlier. I didn't close the door, so it didn't take much to catch me. So, surprise, he knows about us. Don't be mad. You're just so fucking sexy laying here immobilized like this."

"Darla. Can you please fucking explain to me why she's cold to touch but her heart is still beating? I can see it. I can hear it. I want some fucking answers."

Those two love each other. It's why they talk to each other with such… passion.

"Her heart beats. It's slower. She will still be Fallon, but she has changed, Merrick. You need to let her rest. She has been through a lot. We didn't prepare her for this. She will wake up when she's ready."

What. The. Fuck. What has changed?

"Baby girl, I'm sorry I left you too soon. I never wanted to. I thought I got out. That the curse was only a rumor or scare tactic. I was wrong. I should have told you about this place. I should have told you so much. Please don't be mad at me. I'm so sorry."

Daddy, I could never be mad at you.

A shiver crawls up my body. My eyes slowly open, daylight is shining through my window.

Looking down, there's a blanket that isn't my own covering me.

My body feels stiff from laying here for so long. Turning my head to the side, my neck cracks. I haven't moved in days. The rest of my body feels stiff.

I see familiar boots at the edge of the bed. My eyes move up his jean-clad legs, his folded hands are folded on top of his stomach, he's twiddling his thumbs. Continuing up his body, he turns his head to face me. A smirk is on his lips, and his dark eyes take me in.

"She lives."

CHAPTER 28
MERRICK

"**W**hose blanket is this?"

That's the first thing she says after being out for five days. This girl and her priorities.

"Mine. From my room."

She cuddles into it more. "I did wonder why I could smell you so strongly the entire time. That makes sense."

"You are a twisted little girl, aren't you?" Smirking at her while shaking my head in disbelief.

She looks at me confused, "What? Your blanket is so soft. I like it. I'm going to keep it, I think."

"Sure. Keep it. But aren't you at all curious about what the fuck happened... five days ago?"

Fallon seems taken aback by my question. "It's

been five days? It only felt like a couple of hours, maybe. Shit."

Her eyes close, absorbing what I've told her while taking a deep breath, steadying herself.

Nodding her head, she opens her eyes again and releases her deep inhale. "Yeah. Wow. Ok. Don't tell anyone else I'm up? I'm going to shower and change. Then you can tell me everything, before I see anyone else. Please, Merrick."

"Of course." I agree without hesitation. I don't blame her. I'm an insensitive prick, but I can understand how this would be completely overwhelming.

Fallon gets up from bed, slowly. Stretching her limbs, arms over her head, "This feels so good."

She's still in her dress from the ceremony, and her ass is begging for me to bite it through the lace train.

"Merrick. No." She scolds me, which makes me chuckle. My stupid little girl knows me all too well.

Taking careful steps, she makes her way to the door and opens it before leaving, she looks back at me. "I'll be quick," then she leaves the room.

Quick, my ass.

Forty-five fucking minutes is not quick. I get she

had dried blood coating her body, but shit, this is insane.

The door opens, breaking my thoughts. About fucking time.

Fallon is in an oversized white tee, her wavy hair hanging damp over her shoulders.

Jumping on the bed next to me, she crosses her legs. "Ok. Lay it on me. I'm ready."

"Did you touch yourself in the shower?"

"No, Merrick, I just showered. Now is not the time for this." She spits back at me. Fuck, that did not come out right.

"Your skin. Have you touched it?" I throw back at her, rephrasing my question. She looks at me puzzled. "Yes. I cleaned myself… why? What's wrong with it?" She asks while she examines her body.

"Nothing obvious. But it's cold to the touch. I thought you were dying. Or dead. As the days went on, it never warmed up. But your heart kept beating. It didn't make sense." Touching her exposed leg, it still feels cool. Even after her warm shower. So I continue, "Darla says your heart's slower now, much slower. Which is why your skin feels cool. Your blood isn't flowing as fast as it did before the ceremony. She seemed like she was talking to you while you were asleep, or talking to someone else I couldn't see. Darla said you would be fine. That parts of you have changed, but you would still be Fallon."

Fallon's face still seems confused, but she doesn't speak. She simply waits for me to continue.

"So, she wasn't talking to you then. It must have been an elder in the spirit world. They don't always like showing themselves to strangers. Darla has gathered a lot of information while you were out. She said once you're up, everything will make sense. Your dad has been around, too. Safe to say the secrets out that we are fucking. He wasn't thrilled, but he seems to accept it now. So that's exciting for us. Joanie is still dead. Her body was handled and isn't in the graveyard. This way, her spirit can't interfere. She is gone forever. Darla put a curse over her corpse, then Harper and her dad did the rest. Harper has been eager to see you. So if you could handle that, please. Because she is really fucking annoying. But since she's your friend, I've been good. So yeah, welcome back! Also, that levitating trick you did was fucking hot."

Fallon grabs her pillow and whacks me with it across the face.

"You would think five days of sleep would be good for you. But someone still seems a bit testy."

"Merrick. Be nice to Harper, she is my best friend

202

and isn't going anywhere. I want to see my dad. And Darla. Can you get them for me, please?" Fallon's bottom lip pouts and she gives me those puppy dog eyes.

Hello afterlife, I'm Merrick, and I am whipped. Because that's all it takes.

I pop out of her room to the library where Darla and Mark have been spending their days lately.

"Guys. She's up and wants to see the both of you." I snap my fingers and point at both of them.

They both look over at me with wide eyes. I don't stay for the rest of their reaction and head back to Fallon's room.

"They are on their way, milady."

CHAPTER 29

DARLA

U s spirits rarely violate the privacy or the home of our keeper and protector, but unusual circumstances call for unusual measures.

Fallon is sitting on her bed with Merrick, while Mark and I stand at the edge of her bed.

She is the first to speak. "Is that how the ceremonies usually go?"

Her question is valid.

"No, my child. It was the first of its kind that I have seen."

"Why? What happened?" She is confused. Just as I was. Until I wasn't.

"The elder spirits recognized your pure intentions. They also knew you'd been thrown into this, and instead of running or trying to escape the town, you stayed. Where Joanie was evil, you were good. You wanted to learn and understand us, and our town's traditions. I'm sure you were scared or nervous, but you never let it deter you. You never let Merrick deter you. All of this means a lot to us, and the founding elders decided to give you a gift."

"A gift? What do you mean?" Fallon questions.

"My child. The founding elders cast a very special and very rare incantation upon you."

"A fuck what now?" Merrick, ever so charming, speaks up.

"Incantation. Spell. Gift. If you were to cut yourself, you will see that you will bleed blue instead of red. Your skin is now cool to touch because they have slowed your heart rate down. Your energy and health will always remain at its peak. You will never be sick or diseased, and you will never age. In ten years, when you look in the mirror, you will still look as you are today."

"What? Why? I don't understand."

"My child. They have chosen you to have this. They know you will succeed and do great things for this town and the spirits you keep. You will restore the Knight name as one of the founding families. They wanted to thank you, and this is their way of doing so. Eternal health and youth. For as long as you want it. When the time comes and you are ready to pass this duty on and leave the human world, you say the word and they will make it seamless and painless for you. Then you will join us in the spirit world. Your best friend is smart. This was always your fate and destiny, and you embraced it with open arms. Don't think they don't see how Harper has as well. She has something special waiting for her when her time comes, but her ceremony will involve a lot less death. We don't like killing our elders. We have only done it once before, and only when it's necessary. This was. Joanie was toxic. The spirits couldn't be in their form in the cemetery and always had to hide. An uneasy atmosphere, would be a polite way of describing it. But that is in the past. We thank you, Fallon."

Mark speaks up, "Don't be scared, my girl. You are so strong."

Tears well in Fallon's eyes. Merrick grabs her hand and places it in his, comforting her while she takes this all in for the first time.

The founding elders speak through me, and I relay their message. "They said the lights and levitation were for effect. They thought it would be a fun show for the people, and they apologize if it scared you.

Your five days of rest were needed as your body changed."

She faintly laughs. "Fuck. I want to say thank you, but I also want to scream. I know I didn't ask for any of this, but I won't run from it. I'm not a coward. I just need time. To adjust. This is… a lot."

Nodding my head, "I understand, my child. We will give you all the time you need."

Mark and I walk toward her bedroom door when she speaks up once more. "Darla, Dad. You guys can stay in the house or come and go as you please as much as you like. I like having you both around. It's comforting. I've never had more than just my dad, and now I have you, my dad, and Merrick. I want… I need my family around me, please."

Both Mark and I nod our heads.

She will do marvelously.

CHAPTER 30
MERRICK

We are giving Fallon time to adjust.

Two new arrivals have landed in the cemetery since the ceremony, a car accident outside of town. No one claimed the bodies, so we took them in. This happens from time to time.

Some are accidental. Some want to reside here in their afterlife so they do what I did… just on the edge of town. If no one claims them, we will. Fallon needs to help them transition, it's her duty. Explaining the do's and don'ts and making them feel comfortable. Darla is helping for now, but we need to get Fallon out there to take over.

Soon.

Harper was over for like three fucking hours

talking her ear off. I had to leave and smoke a joint in my room. It was too much.

Harper is another one that I think, do you ever stop? Is there an off switch? Fucking energizer bunny, that one is.

Fallon showed off her new party trick, though, the blue blood baddie that she is.

Harper loved it. As Harper would.

The first few days after everything, Fallon was still slowly absorbing it all, and was less vocal than normal. Which was alarming since she's usually shouting at me for something. She spent time with her dad, and they would spend all night talking some evenings. It's not like he's been dead long. Fuck if I know what they could be catching up on.

It must be a daddy daughter thing?

It doesn't bother me, it's just... What do you talk about for that long?

I couldn't imagine talking to Joanie for more than fourteen seconds.

Ding dong, the bitch is dead! So that point is irrelevant.

Anyway, since Harper left, Fallon, my little minx, has been trying to break into my room.

I can't call her my stupid little girl anymore...

She's fucking superhuman now and could probably kick my ass. I'm testing new ones out to avoid that.

I've tried calling her my kinky gopher nipples, my tight pussy, and my dirty devil. All three she has shut down and absolutely hated.

So now, she is my little minx, but don't worry folks, she will always be my desperate little slut in bed. She is what she eats, and she begs for my cock regardless of her mental state.

The doorknob falls to the floor.

What the fuck.

This isn't her first attempt, but it is the first time she's gotten this far.

She pushes the door open and walks in, pride written all over her face. Smiling ear to ear and dropping her handyman tools to the ground.

"You're impressed, right?"

I'm leaning against my windowsill, slow clapping for her. "You did it. You killed the doorknob."

"You're such an asshole," she mumbles while checking out my space. It's dusty as fuck. I don't clean, I'm not sure if you have noticed, but I don't exactly scream molly fucking maid, do I? But the room is the same as it was when I died. A couple of posters of hot chicks with cars are on my wall, some sports shit on my shelves from my dad; with a few books, a dresser and desk making the room up, along with the bed.

"It's not what I expected." My little minx announces.

"Oh?" My eyebrows raise.

"Yeah, I thought maybe it would look more like Satan's lair. More flames and horns and less of this."

"Sorry to disappoint. It is a normal room. With a normal view of the Angel of Death."

She goes to speak, but I stop her before she can. "Wait, let me guess. Such an asshole?" Fallon laughs. It's exactly what she was going to say.

Popping up behind her, I wrap my fingers around her neck. "I'll show you asshole." I kick the door closed with my foot, and it slams shut.

Letting go of her briefly, I turn into my spirit form and grab her throat again with my hand. This time lifting her up and throwing her body against the door, a loud bang echoes in the room as her body connects with the hard wooden door and she falls to the floor.

Walking to stand in front of her, I show myself again. She is getting up while on all fours, but freezes when she sees my boots in front of her and she looks up at me.

"Stay. Down." I instruct as I begin undoing my pants. Her chest heaves with anticipation, and she looks up at me through her long eyelashes while biting her lip.

"Take my boots off, slut."

She obeys.

Unlacing them and sliding them off my feet, Fallon places them off to the side and resumes her previous position on all fours.

I slide my pants off and remove my shirt. My cock is hard and dripping precum.

"Are you hungry, my desperate little slut?" I question, while rubbing my thumb along the tip of my cock. "You want this? You want to choke on me, don't you?"

Looking up through her lashes, she nods her head.

Going into my spirit form, I bend down and grab her neck. Raising her up so she's on her knees. Her mouth opens and her tongue sticks out. "Such a good, desperate slut." I praise her and show myself again. I let go of her and shove my cock into her mouth and down her throat.

She gags instantly, fucking music to my ears.

I love when she gags on me. Moving my hips, I force myself further down her throat. She holds onto my thighs for support, hollowing out her cheeks and she lets me fuck her face. With each movement, she gags more and tears stream down her cheeks, but she is a fucking trooper and doesn't pull back.

She can't breathe. I feel her trying to gasp as her throat milks me with contractions. This is the shit that gets me off. Fallon, completely at my mercy, willingly.

Slapping her cheek, "Such a good slut, gagging on my cock." I don't let up.

Fallon gags again, and I cum instantly. Ropes of my release coat her throat as I work her harder, chasing every moment of my orgasm. My hands are now tangled in her hair as I hold her head in place as I continue to work myself. I give one last thrust into her mouth, and she ends up throwing up all over my dick. It's the hottest thing I've ever seen. I pull myself out of her and vomit runs down the front of her chest. She gasps for air desperately.

I'm hard immediately again.

"You are so fucking beautiful."

Not letting her clean up, my hands still in her hair, I pull her up.

"Take your clothes off."

Removing her shorts first, Fallon kicks them off to the side. I let go of her hair so she can remove her shirt, and she's not even wearing a bra underneath. Desperate little slut.

"Get on the bed. On all fours, facing the headboard."

She takes the back of her hand and wipes her mouth, then winks at me as she walks seductively to my bed.

Her ass is begging for me. I can hear it. *'Fuck me, daddy Merrick. I need your giant cock in my backdoor.'*

I rub my hands together; your wish is my command.

Fallon gets in position. On her hands and knees with her delicious booty facing me, and on my childhood bed. Fuck me. Dreams really do come true.

FALLON

Feeling the bed dip behind me, I know it's Merrick.

His roughness is something I crave. Just when I think it couldn't get any better, it does. A sharp sting against my backside causes me to arch my back. I've never gagged so much I vomited during a blowjob before. So, naturally you would think it would be embarrassing, but it wasn't. It was liberating. He didn't judge either, he fucking loved it.

Together, we are twisted.

We give each other what we need.

His hand grabs onto my long hair, wrapping it around his fist a couple of times, which pulls my head and neck back.

I feel him line his cock up to my hole before he rams into my backside.

A loud moan leaves my mouth, his free hand grabs hold of my neck, and his hips move frantically. "Your ass is taking me so well." Merrick pants from behind me.

He pulls harder on my hair, "You are so fucking desperate. Your pussy is jealous. I can smell it. It's dripping with desperation."

A moan leaves my lips in response. He's right. I need him inside of me everywhere.

He lets go of my hair, my head bends forward and he moves to my breasts. Grabbing hold of one of my nipples, playing with it between his thumb and fore-finger. "Cum," he demands as he squeezes my nipple. It stings perfectly and I feel his warm cum coating my back. He pulled out to decorate me. My pussy tingles with its own release, and my legs tingle. My eyes rolling in ecstasy.

"My little slut likes it when I paint her with my cum, don't you?"

Moaning in response, "Yes, fuck. I need more."

"You are so fucking needy for me. You get what I give you, slut." He pants as I feel him still coating me with his sticky cum.

Merrick lets go of my throat.

Leaning over me, his voice tickles my ear. "My hand print is already leaving a mark. Just how you like it."

He's right. I fucking love his marks on me.

Then, in one quick movement, he flips me over. I'm on my back laying on his bed while he hovers over me, his lips brush against mine. "Fucking perfect."

My tongue is feeling playful, and I lick his lips before nipping them.

His mouth crashes against mine, and he nips me back.

It sends my body into a frenzy. I wrap my legs around his fit waist, and he leans back slightly, "Love you, my stupid little girl."

I laugh at him. He has been testing new nicknames out all week and I guess we are back to this one.

"What's so fucking funny?" He looks at me, confused.

Shaking my head, "Love you too." I say back, sitting up then kissing the tip of his nose. My favorite smirk forms on his face. "Rest. We have a busy night ahead."

He disappears, only to reappear a moment later with his blanket in hand. It's been in my room since he covered me with it after the ceremony and he isn't getting it back.

Merrick covers me with it, tucking me in. It's really sweet how his soft side has come out for me.

Don't worry, it's only sometimes. With everyone else, he is still an asshole.

CHAPTER 31
MERRICK

S he's been sleeping for a few hours, and I am bored out of my fucking mind. I do love watching her sleep, though. When she's dreaming, her little nose crunches, and it's so fucking cute. But we need to wake her ass up.

Grabbing her shoulders, I start shaking her. "FALLON WAKE UP!"

Her eyes shoot open, and she is scared shitless. She starts screaming and grabs onto my arms. It's fucking hilarious.

Once she realizes I am only messing with her, I let go of her and brace for impact. My girl doesn't miss a beat and begins punching my shoulder. "You. Fucking. Asshole."

I'm laughing hysterically. She's pissed.

Fallon lets up and gives me 'I would kill you if you aren't already dead' eyes.

"Get dressed. You have new spirits to welcome, and Darla has been smothering them. You have to save them from her annoying fucking rambles."

She lets out a big sigh. She knows it's fucking time. We haven't pushed her, but it's time to nudge now.

"You're right about getting out of here. It's time and I'm ready. Not about Darla, though. She doesn't ramble."

"Good. Now get dressed. I'll meet you out there." I tell her and kiss her cheek before disappearing.

Twenty-eight minutes.

My guys, talk to me. What takes these ladies so fucking long to put on clothes? I can only wear the same shit every day, it's a ghost thing. It only takes me a minute or two to put mine back on after I fuck my girl into coma.

What the fuck are their clothes made of that it takes them twenty-eight fucking minutes to put them on and walk back here?

This needs to go on that show about unsolved

mysteries, because I'm not sure we will ever be able to solve this puzzle.

My head turns towards the entrance when I hear branches snap.

Standing up, I see she's in a pair of chucks, sweatpants and a long sleeve henley. My long sleeve henley. I know that shit isn't unsolvable. You put it over your head and slide your arms in.

"Cold feet?" I throw out there. She shakes her head, "No. I was getting dressed. Not all of us can pop in and out."

"Right, but eternal health and youth are normal." I joke back at her. She shakes her head at me, smiling.

"Darla. Stop annoying those poor new spirits and get over here." I shout out into the night sky. "Merrick, you are such a little shit." And there she is, the side of Darla only I can bring out.

"Merrick, be nice," Fallon scolds. These two team up all the time now. They have some sort of fucking sisterhood or some shit. Even Mark gets it from them. No one is safe with these two.

I throw my hands up in surrender, it's the safest course of action. Unless you know you can win, and I know I won't win this one.

"So, my child, how does it feel?" she asks Fallon.

She looks around, taking it all in like it's the first

time. "Yeah, it feels good. Like it's where I'm meant to be. My soul is screaming, this is its home."

"Good. Now, let's go introduce you to your two new spirits. They are nervous, but excited. You will need to go over the rules, the town, and most importantly, make them feel comfortable. A happy spirit is a happy town. The town needs to stay happy. It's October, we are open to the public and we don't need drama getting out." Darla turns to face me. "And Merrick, don't get them worked up. So help me, boy."

"Darla, I'm insulted." I act hurt, holding my heart.

"Let's go then, our little saint." She says back to me as she walks deeper into the cemetery.

I reach my hand out to Fallon, who grabs onto it.

"You will never be in this alone." I promise her.

"Good. I need your smart ass with me through all of this." She smiles up at me.

MERRICK

EPILOGUE

Yup. It happened. Karma came, and it said open up, Merrick, because I have a treat for you.

And I bent over and let it fuck me.

At first, I didn't think I would like it. But it turns out I really do.

I'm a dad.

I'm a dad to a three-year-old girl who could ramble at me for hours and I'll listen.

Yeah, that's right. This ghost dick can procreate.

We are in the town on the last day it's open before Halloween. My kid, who is dressed up like a daisy, is running around like she just ingested a bag of sugar. I fucking love it.

Her aunt Harper made her the costume. Good

news is she didn't use her dead mom as the model. So that's a nice change.

We are at the clock tower, tourists are taking loads of pictures and a few are lined up for ghost tours.

Darla brought the idea up to Fallon a couple of years ago. They had done it in the past, but Joanie pissed the spirits off so much they stopped participating in the tours. So they were canceled.

To say the least, shit was bad under Joanie. Shit is fucking rainbows under my lady. Fallon is doing a great fucking job.

The spirits all adore her. She's kind and caring. Helps them navigate their journey and keeps their home in the cemetery a peaceful place to be.

Anyway, Fallon hired a few of the local teens to do the tours. The spirits get to play and scare the shit out of the tourists. Although, there is this one motherfucker who comes each year who pisses me off. He never startles or shows any sign of fear on the tour.

I have made it my personal mission to make him piss his pants this year.

He waited until tonight to come.

I have it all planned. This time on the tour, I won't even bother. He is expecting it. It's a game. This time I am waiting until he gets in his piece of shit car.

Where I'll be hiding. He will pull out of his spot and head to the bridge out of town.

That's when I'll pop up in front of his moving car. I'll throw myself onto his windshield.

Oh no, he has killed a man.

As he is standing over me, freaking the fuck out, I'll open my eyes and yell, "Boo, are you scared yet?" Then I'll disappear.

Guaranteed pant pissing. Or a heart attack. Both are acceptable. I chuckle to myself thinking about it. That's for later. Fucker won't even know what hit em.

"Hails, stay close to us, please." I shout at my daughter, who is weaving in and around people.

Fallon's hand is in mine, as her other hand holds her rounding stomach.

Yes, karma said you will have two daughters. Two daughters who will eventually have synced cycles with their beautiful mother. I couldn't be more excited if I tried.

"You're telling them about the girls, aren't you?" Fallon questions, smirking.

"Yeah. And how blessed we are to have been gifted with two tiny princesses."

She laughs at me. Fallon also knows my karma theory and doesn't dispute it. She fucking loves it, actually.

Winking at me, "Such an asshole."

We aren't married. We didn't feel the need to get married.

I put my super ghost sperm inside of her and it created a tiny human. That was me publicly claiming her. Which means a fuck load more to me than a fucking ring on a finger and scripted vows.

Now I know the question on everyone's mind is… is the donut dick still on the driveway?

The answer is yes. Yes, it is folks!

Mark tried to scrub it off when we told him he was going to be a grandpa, but that shit is on there good.

Hails has seen it when playing on the second-floor balcony. She said, "Daddy, what is that?" with a slight tilt to her cute little blonde haired head. The blonde was alarming at first, since we are both naturally dark haired. But my super ghost sperm took my bleached white hair and put that in my kid. Which is kind of sweet.

I explained to her that before Mommy killed Grandma Joanie—you know Joanie is cringing at being called grandma—that daddy took mommy's car and used the tires to make a cool picture on the drive-way. Grandma Joanie didn't appreciate art, though, and she got really mad.

"But what is it?" And I would never lie to my child, so I told her. A donut penis.

Fallon walked out in that exact moment, mortified. She didn't flip out, but she was not happy.

I explained to Fallon later that we really dodged a bullet there. Hails could have asked why Mommy killed grandma Joanie?

Could you fucking imagine? I can't wait for the day when she does ask. I'll tell her the epic story of that fateful night.

So in short. Yes, the donut dick is still on the driveway.

Mark is actually a really good grandpa. He loves hanging out with the kid. They spend hours playing in the cemetery.

Harper is still Harper. I think she talks more since shacking up with her new guy, if that's even possible. Fallon and Harper won't tell me who the guy is. I've tried to sneak in when they are talking, but Fallon can feel me as soon as I enter in my spirit form, and they immediately stop talking.

In other news related to Harper, they finally buried her mom. That only took ten years. I haven't seen her yet, but Fallon says she's still adjusting and needs more space to process it all.

That's all I got.

I'm going to go enjoy the rest of the night with my kid and woman before I need to head out and scare that motherfucker once and for all.

You've got our story. Now fuck off.

"Daddy, say please." Hails stomps her foot at me.

"Sorry about that, Hails. Now, please fuck off. Is that better?"

Smiling back at me, "Yes. Thank you, daddy."

You heard the girl.

Now, please fuck off.

THE END

This pussy tight like a nun... this song had to have been inspired by Fallon. Because that is exactly how her pussy feels. You could never tell she's had my PhD in her 24/7 and a human head slide out of her. Kegels.

Now it's The fucking End.

Fuck Me, Daddy; A Port Canyon Chronicle
Coming Eventually.

ACKNOWLEDGMENTS

Daddy Ghost Dick has been in my head since the fall of 2022! Merrick was the first book I ever thought of writing as I was debating to enter the author world. I mean, I had book ideas as a kid, but those don't count. They were most likely horrendous and involved too much sunshine and not enough darkness.

Moving on…His and Fallon's story came to me in a dream one night. After waking up from it, I immediately opened a fresh doc and wrote the idea down. There was no way I was forgetting this. Yes, he has always been this way; no filter, no bullshit, all fun and chaos. And in my eyes, he is perfection. I fucking adore him. My excitement over him is borderline annoying at this point, but I don't care. He is my first book idea. Which I always knew would be released to the world on Friday, October 13.

The wait was torture, but now it's finally time.

In case you're wondering, Joanie was always a cunt and had to go. The house slightly resembles my dream house. And Mark is indeed, K.L. Taylor-Lane's husband's name. Shout out to Mark. Congrats Gramps – haha. He hates when I call him that.

The rumors are true, I have never been ghost dicked myself. So I could only describe it how I felt it would be like it. For those of you who have, I hope I did it justice.

Fun Fact: The ladies of Slide Between the Pages Podcast informed me that, getting GD is more common than we think. When you choke on your own spit, you know what I mean. It is also a form of getting Ghost Dicked. Who knew, right? The more you know.

But I digress!

I hope you all enjoyed Ghost Dick!

Wait! Another Fun Fact: This book was originally called Her Ghost, with a different cover and graphics ready to go by 3 Crows Author Services. A week or two before I announced this project, I knew it didn't feel right. I never called it Her Ghost in my head or when talking about it. I always called it Ghost Dick.

So, urgently one morning, I called upon Haaaaannnnnaaaah and said, if I needed a cover done, here is the concept here is the name, what would you say?

Thank fuck, she said yes to the dress! She also nailed it with the promo graphics.

Yes! Fuck Me, Daddy: A Port Canyon Chronicle. Release date TBD. Fallon and Merrick will totally make an appearance.

With all that said, I know I have no business writing PNR, but here we are. If there are rules and I didn't follow them, my bad. Even if I knew some of the rules, we all know now that Merrick wouldn't follow them anyways. Thank you for reading Ghost Dick!

To the readers, my warriors and Queens! THANK YOU for reading me. THANK YOU for supporting me. This year has been a trip, in the best possible way, all because of you. I wish I could be on KU for you to read. Maybe one day us taboo authors can be. Until that day comes, know I appreciate every eBook and paperback you purchase. Along with every post, video, recommendation and DM. I'm soo excited to bring you more crazy, dark and delicious taboo reads in the coming years! Thank you and I love you all!

Hannnnaaaahhhh, oh Haaaaannnaaahhh. I will forever be grateful for having you in my life as a friend and as this creative genius who humors my ideas. You spoil me with your kindness. You were my first character/book edit; Within the Shadows. Which I now have on a canvas, hanging on my wall. Thank you for everything and I cannot wait for everything to come that we have planned together! I love you!!

My ARC and Street Team! Y'all are next level and I am obsessed. And the fact that you want to help me? This taboo author? I appreciate each and every one of you. Your support, your excitement, the shares and everything you do. I value more than words can express. Thank you will have to do for now.

Amanda! Thank you for being my PA. And knowing come Monday I have usually gone rogue that Sunday and you just go with the flow of it. This is only the beginning of our journey but I am excited to see where it takes us.

My Alpha and Betas! Often you will say that you are questioning your morals reading what I have written. Thank you for allowing me to do that and not running away. Your commentary while reading the stories make my life. I appreciate each one of you for taking the time out of your lives to help me. Thank you!!!!

Ra Ra Reads as my husband calls you. The crafty book witch as we know her! Thank you for editing

GD and taking care of my babies. Even if you may not fully admit it, you love Merrick. It's fine. But know, I know – haha

Mr. Kincaid. This is another one where you will think, '*Where the fuck does she get these ideas?*' And as I always respond back, just let it happen. It is easier that way. Thank you for supporting me and my dreams. For not minding my endless nights typing away. So much of this wouldn't be possible without you. Thank you for putting up with me and wifey, KL. And for giving us laughs when you go on some random rant! Love you dearest!!

K, wifey, sister from another mister, the lady O to my Gayle. I love you. You are my favorite. I seriously could go on for days about it, but I will spare you all from the sappy, I love you, no I love you, back and forth - haha. K, from the hours of endless laugher to just talking things out, I enjoy every minute of it. Thank you for always cheering me on and for being my sounding board. We may write different tropes but this journey is a shared one between us. It always feels like we are two twisted but strong females, supporting and lifting each other up, every chance we get. It is something I think is rare in female friendships and something I cherish deeply. I wouldn't want to share any of this with anyone else. With that said, one of my many thank yous include, gifting you the ability to say, you have a book title on your shelf called *Fuck Me, Daddy.* I know, I am the gift that just keeps on giving. What can I say other than, I am at your service. Seriously though, I love you and thank you for being in my life. I am keeping you!

That is it. That is all.

Thank you for reading Ghost Dick Daddy Merrick!

Until the next one,

-Kins

ABOUT THE AUTHOR

Kinsley is a Canadian, Taboo Dark Romance Author. When she isn't plotting her next twisted book or watching true crime docs with her cats, you can find her working for the man. Reading. Or drinking wine… vodka… beer… while causing chaos with friends, let's not limit ourselves now. Make sure you follow Kins on her socials and sign up for her newsletter to see what is coming next!

Kinsley Kincaid's Website

MORE FROM THE AUTHOR

FORBIDDEN

Let's Play - Freebie

Within the Shadows

Lessons from the Depraved - Feb 2024

TABOO

Wrecked

Sutton Asylum

Dark Temptation: Part One - Freebie

Ghost Dick

Dark Temptation: Part Two – Christmas 2023

Sick Obsession - 2024

www.ingramcontent.com/pod-product-compliance
Lightning Source LLC
Chambersburg PA
CBHW061446070425
24705CB00036B/706